THE NAKED FLESH

WOLFBAIT
UNDER THE COUNTER CULTURE

First published in 1962 The Naked Flesh
This edition published in 2026
by Wolfbait Books
www.wolfbait.co.uk
All rights reserved © 2026.

Cover design: Scott Sugiuchi
www.scottsugiuchi.com

A CIP record for this book is available from
the British Library
ISBN: 978-1-917298-12-4 (paperback)
ISBN: 978-1-917298-13-1 (ebook)

THE NAKED FLESH

by Orrie Hitt

FOREWORD

SKIN, SIN, AND sun. What more could a pulp or mystery writer want from a setting? Since the 1930s, fictional nudist camps have attracted more than a few authors. Peter Hunt, for instance, kills off a nudist woman by electrocution in his *Murder Among the Nudists* (1934), and gives Inspector Alan Miller only the barest of clues to find the killer. Traill Stevenson opens *The Nudist Murder* (1937) with the discovery near a nudist camp of a strangled naked woman and ties her death to a nudist photographer bent on revenge. In E. R. Punshon's *Death Among the Sunbathers* (1955), police trace the shooting of a female journalist to a 'fanatical' group of sunbathers.

Pulp and mystery writers such as these have shown an unnerving creativity in placing criminal activity in nudist settings. Naked bodies are found in nudist camp swimming pools; nudist club owners blackmail guests with surreptitious photographs; others secretly prostitute young women in what is advertised as a family-friendly environment. Often, what looks like a chaste setting is all part of a money-grubbing racket with libertine sex—or so the pulps say.

What is it that draws so many pulp and mystery writers to nudism? The novelty and sensual allure of naked female bodies are the obvious answers, but the reasons are more complex.

People have long enjoyed skinny-dipping and nude sunbathing at secluded beaches, swimming holes, and hot springs. Still, nudism remains a fascinating mystery, and authors since the 1930s have found it just as intriguing and mystifying as their readers.

Nudist settings provide an ideal backdrop for crime in fiction. In the 1930s, when organised nudism first splashed across British and American newspapers, the public could hardly read enough about the fad. Nudists seemed a strange and peculiar lot. Social nudity was a mystery itself and connoted sexual intrigue, disreputable camp owners, crackpots, and scam artists. No one quite knew what went on behind the walls of the 'nudist colony' outside of town. The world of nudism was alien to most, while criminal activity thrown into the mix exaggerated the fascination with the environment.

Writers from the 1930s through to today have thus repeatedly bludgeoned, stabbed, shot, strangled, electrocuted, poisoned, drowned, or otherwise done in their naked victims in nudist settings. Those left alive were blackmailed, conned out of money, prostituted, or otherwise socially ruined. The hint of a crime made a mystery; set in a nudist camp—many publishers thought—made it a marketable mystery.

Nudism's most obvious draw to mystery and pulp writers is its perceived obscurity, sexuality, and danger. Organised nudism—perhaps more than the practice of mere skinny-dipping and sunbathing at a secluded beach—is largely unknown to most readers. Everyone has heard of nudist camps, clubs, or 'colonies', but few have firsthand experience with the goings-on there. The walls, gates, and secretive memberships of most nudist camps lend an air of clandestine 'otherness' to nudists. Whether or not camps prohibit the public from visiting their grounds, the perception in many non-nudists' minds is that activity at a nudist club is as enigmatic as life on another planet. Stories placed in nudist settings thus have a heightened intrigue.

Nudist camps were and usually remain today well outside urban areas. Many were set in hard-to-find locales and used fencing or natural barriers to keep gawkers from peeking into camp life. The seclusion of nudist camps and their desire to avoid public view added to nudism's sense of intrigue. Many clubs scrutinised visitors before admitting them onto the grounds. This, too, exaggerated the notion that nudist camps were secretive organisations, and thus prime settings for criminal schemes.

The cloistered environment of nudist camps provided an additional bonus to mystery writers. With nudists being so secretive, and with clubs limiting the number of their members, one could assume that everyone at a nudist club would know their associates; and since they were nude, men and women could be portrayed as knowing each other rather intimately, and perhaps sexually.

On the other hand, fictional nudists often followed the real-life practice in nudism's early years of using only first names and of not inquiring about the lives of others outside the club. This allowed writers to portray individual nudists as having criminal lives unknown to their naked peers. Nudist settings therefore provided the social intimacy and personal relationships requisite for criminal action, while giving the author the means of keeping important details of a suspect's life hidden from other characters.

In a conceptual disconnect, many non-nudists also equate 'Eden-like' social nudity with sexual liberty, giving crime in a nudist setting a marketable eroticism. Some publishers played up the purported sexual angle of social nudity. For instance, each of the original covers for Orrie Hitt's pulp novels set in part at a nudist camp features an attractive naked woman.

Publishers understood their readers' fascination with nudism and often exaggerated a story's tie to it. The front and back covers of William L. Rohde's *Murder on the Line* (1951) make it sound like the entire novel is set in a nudist camp. As it is, the novel contains only one chapter in which railroad detective Mohawk Daniels searches for a female murder suspect at a camp. The nudist setting has nothing to do with the story and simply provides an opportunity for readers to follow Daniels naked as he chases an equally naked woman across the grounds.

Nudist settings are also perceived as dangerous. If people are willing to run about naked illegally with strangers, then they will likely be willing to break other laws. Nudists are thus perceived as morally ambiguous and as living on society's borderlands.

Murder, moreover, is only one of many dire threats nudist clubs purportedly pose. In both Stevenson's *The Nudist Murder* and Norman Longmate's *Strip Death Naked*, visitors to nudist settings are photographed surreptitiously and then blackmailed. Hitt follows suit with each of his three nudist novels. In Gillian Linscott's *A Healthy Body* (1984), a French nudist resort is the setting for drug smuggling. Rape, as well as the possibility of murder, is the danger in Heather Macintyre's pornographic crime novel, *The Captive Nudist* (1978).

If nudist camps were alien to most people, the idea of running one as a business appeared particularly suspicious. Pulp fiction portrayed nudist entrepreneurs as criminals defrauding their club members or using the camp as a front for prostitution or a haven for mob couriers. Where mysteries aim to entertain readers by presenting puzzles requiring attention to detail and inductive reasoning, pulp fiction tends to satisfy appetites for mere erotic or violent spectacle.

Orrie Hitt's protagonists in his nudist pulp novels find themselves in clothes-free settings they initially take as potential hotbeds of sexual bedlam. And there are ample numbers of bare bosoms and aching female loins to keep the central male figures suitably entertained. But the nudists within the novels are presented as honest, though quirky, men and women seeking full exposure to the sun for physical and social health. Hitt made one clothed visit to a nudist camp for research purposes and read various nudist magazines to give him that much insight. But then the supposed criminal underbelly of social nudity arises, and the noirish themes so popular with pulp have their licentious day in the sun.

Hitt's trifecta of nudist flesh will do little to educate readers regarding mid-century US nudism, but they continue to delight our lower brows.

Mark Storey
Author of *Cinema au Naturel: A History of Nudist Film*

1

DUTCH GOT UP from the bed and walked across the hotel room to the window. Going to the window was a waste of time. All he could see was the blank wall of a building next door and the warm April sun that spilled down into the alley with most of the rays somehow getting lost before they reached the street level.

Of course his given name wasn't Dutch but everybody called him that and he didn't mind. The Lands had come from Holland generations before him so it was perfectly natural that nobody called him Harry. He didn't mind that either; he wasn't happy over the name of Harry. No reason. Just that he didn't care for it.

He was a big man, a couple of inches over six feet, and he weighed a hundred and eighty pounds. None of his weight was fat. He was all raw muscle and bone with broad shoulders and close cut sandy hair. As for being handsome he didn't know. He grinned and turned from the window. Most of the women thought he was pretty much of a man at the age of twenty-six and that, to Dutch, was what counted.

Still grinning, he regarded the girl lying on the bed. She was nude, her small breasts tired in the light of morning, her eyes closed as she slept. He had only met her the night before and wasn't too clear about the circumstances. There had been that bar, a few drinks with her when he should have quit drinking and her request for twenty dollars. He hadn't been with an American girl in two years and the price had seemed to be cheap enough. The funny part was that he'd paid her and he hadn't done anything in the bed except sleep. He dressed quietly and he didn't disturb the sleeping girl. There was no desire inside of him for her, just some kind of a pity that he didn't quite understand.

At ten o'clock, leaving the sleeping girl behind him, he left the hotel and walked down the street. He carried nothing. All that he owned had gone ahead on the train that he'd missed the night before. It didn't worry him any. People knew him in Cranston and they'd hold the luggage for him.

He felt the heat but that, he supposed, was to be expected. Even in April it was hotter in the city that it had ever gotten in Iceland. Given time, you got used to the climate up there and when the temperature hit sixty degrees you stripped to your T-shirt.

The next train didn't leave until evening—Cranston was too small a place for regular service—and he had nothing to do other than sit at some bar. That was all right with Dutch. Iceland had very few bars and only one sold beer. He'd gone there frequently but there were always fights and an American had to be careful that he didn't use his fists on a native. The girls were a different story. They didn't care who pleased them as long as they got what they wanted. Few of them went without.

He crossed the street and entered a bar. While he'd worked on that pile of rocks he'd thought about the city, wanting to get back to it, but in less than twenty-four hours he was already tired of the whole thing. He had also thought of going home but he couldn't guess what he'd do after he got there. His parents were dead, the farm deserted, and Penny was married. Blonde Penny, he decided, was a sore memory for him. He'd gone away because of her marriage but he didn't blame her too much for that any more. He'd loved her and he hadn't touched her but she'd given herself to Cliff Horton once too often and she'd been forced to make the kid legal.

"Beer," he told the bartender.

"Bottle?"

"Does it matter?"

He paid for the beer but he didn't drink any of it right away. Two years out of the states had changed things for him. He was harder than before, more deliberate in his thinking, but he didn't have the faintest idea what he was going to do with the farm. Selling it appeared to be the wisest choice. There was a lot of land with a good lake but the soil on top of Park Mountain had never produced near what the people got off the low sections along the river.

The bar was small and he was the only customer—for the moment.

He heard her come in and he studied her with interest as she sat down on a stool and ordered a screwdriver. Young. About twenty, possibly a year older. Black hair that was matched by her black dress. A flat stomach from what he could tell and high, thrusting breasts. She would hit forty or forty-two inches there and if the dress had any less material she'd be outside of it. The idea appealed to him but he told himself that he didn't want somebody for money. Paying cash for flesh always ruined it for him.

"I'm buying," he said.

The girl turned her head to look at him. He hadn't taken particular notice of her face and it rather surprised him. It was the kind of a face that should be on a magazine cover. She had dark, curious eyes, a small nose, full, red lips that hesitated and then returned his smile.

"Thanks," she said.

"You're welcome."

He picked up his bottle and glass and moved down to sit beside the girl. It was the same old pitch. You met a girl, bought her a few drinks and maybe you got something from her and maybe you didn't. He guessed it was a chance that any wandering male took.

"A screwdriver," she told the bartender. She had a low, sensual voice.

Dutch threw a twenty on the bar. He had a lot of twenties, both in his wallet and on deposit in the bank in Cranston. He hadn't worked in Iceland for nothing and a buck up there stretched like a rubber band where a fellow played in the black market. A fifth of liquor that cost a dollar and a half through the company could be sold for nine dollars in Icelandic money.

"You haven't got any color in your face," the girl said.

"Well, I wasn't in Florida all winter."

"In jail?"

"One of my own making."

"I don't follow you."

"I've been out of the country. Iceland. For two years. I just got back yesterday."

"Vacation?"

"No. The job was finished. They've got another project in Turkey but I've got no yen for that. I may spend the next few months fishing."

"You must have made some money."

"Maybe."

They drank and talked. Her name was Cherry Graves, she was twenty-one and a model.

"Nudes," she said and shrugged. "But I'm getting tired of it. There are too many girls in the field and not enough pay."

His glance wandered over the rich curves of her body. He could imagine her nude, ripe and ready to be known, surrendering her treasures for the enjoyment of the male. For some reason he felt himself being drawn to her and that was unusual. Since Penny he had resisted this feeling, simply using a girl for whatever physical satisfaction he could find. Penny had taught him that it didn't always pay to be a gentleman or at least he had arrived at that conclusion. Perhaps that wasn't fair but after a girl hurt a man he suffered and he lived through hell.

"Nudes," he said. "There must be a market for them."

"Oh, yes."

"Don't you resent posing that way?"

"Not in the least."

He hadn't let himself go with anybody in a long time but he soon found himself doing it with her. He didn't say anything about Penny but he spoke of the farm and how he didn't know what to do with it.

"Is it big?" she wanted to know.

"Around two hundred and fifty acres."

"Water?"

"For drinking? Sure and there's a lake."

"Is it on the main highway?"

"No. It's on a back road and way up on top of a mountain. If I decide to sell locating a buyer may be difficult. As a farm it couldn't be worse but the lake may appeal to somebody from the city."

She seemed interested and she asked him a lot of questions about the place, a great many more questions than the average girl would ask.

"You could make some money up there," she said finally. "A wad of it."

"Look, I haven't got any gold mine."

She toyed with her drink, then swung on her stool to face him. Those cannons she had in front plunged forward against the dress and the top was low enough so he could see the start of her cleavage.

"A nudist colony is legal in your state," she said.

"What's that got to do with me?"

"People go to them."

"I've heard they did."

"I go myself."

"Well, if they photograph you in the nude it wouldn't bother you any. Personally, I've never seen any sense to it except that it takes away the mystery about sex. Up in Iceland men and women often swim together in the raw and think nothing of what they're doing. It's the same with the native girls. Down here you might buy a girl a drink after a movie but she could be offended if you asked her to spend the night with you. An Icelandic girl wouldn't be offended. It's a common practice and just because she sleeps with you doesn't mean there's any physical relationship during the night. Rape is almost unheard of on the island. It may be due to the fact that they have a broader viewpoint of what to many of us is a forbidden subject."

"Almost like one big nudist camp, huh?"

"No, I wouldn't say that. What they do or don't do comes naturally. I know the first time I ran into it I was shocked. I'd stayed at this hotel and in the morning I shaved in the bathroom. There was only one bathroom on the floor and no lock on the door. All of a sudden the door opened and this girl came in. She had on a robe but after she switched on the shower she took the robe off. It didn't disturb her that she was naked or that I was looking at her. All she did was smile and get under the shower."

Cherry Graves laughed.

"Which pleased you, didn't it?"

"Not exactly. I wasn't sure what I should think. Later, after it was explained to me, I knew."

She had another screwdriver and the bartender brought him a bottle of beer.

"It's just the same in a nudist colony," she said.

"Anyway we're all nudists to a certain extent."

"That's possible."

"Take the girl who lives alone and she comes home from work. What's the first thing that she's apt to do?"

"I'm not a girl so I wouldn't know."

"Nine times out of ten she'll kick off her shoes. The shoes are killing her and if she's wearing a griddle that's killing her, too. So she gets out of all that she can and most likely she goes down to nothing. She wants to be comfortable and that's true of a nudist. It's also true that they worship the sun. They aren't wrong in that. There's a lot of value in the sun."

Dutch nodded. He realized this from his stay in Iceland. During the summer if you cut yourself the cut would heal rather quickly but in the winter, when there was hardly any light at all, the cut would linger for twice the normal length of time. Of course fishing was the main industry of the island and dried cod was an important fish. Most people thought that the drying of cod had originated because of a need for food but that was only partly the reason. In the beginning, the resident had recognized the worth of the sun and had attempted to capture the rays of the sun in the summer through hanging the cod outside to dry. Naturally, this had failed to bring about the desired effect but the effort demonstrated that even the people of ancient times had known that men could not live long without the sun.

"Using the farm for that is a thought," he admitted.

Her eyes were frank and honest.

"I'm glad we met," she said.

"So am I."

"You're at loose ends and that makes two of us. I even considered chucking the whole mess and going back home. That's in Pennsylvania. In the coal fields. What I'd do after I got there is anybody's guess."

"A nudist camp would cost money," he said.

"Not too much. You can get off the ground for very little. What your customers want is privacy. That's the important thing."

"I wouldn't know how to start one if it could be done for a dime."

"Not being familiar with the operation I guess you would need help."

"Yeah. But where do you find that kind of help?"

She reached in under her dress and adjusted her bra strap.

"I told you I was fed up with what I've been doing. There's nothing to keep me here in the city."

"I see."

He saw. He saw her up there in that big house and her naked body on a bed. He could feel her lifting to him, her legs demanding as they brought him closer, could feel the flesh fire of her lips.

"Of course if it appeals to you," she said.

"Do you have to have a permit or something?"

"Not where you live."

"Where do you get the people?"

The bartender fired her another screwdriver.

"I've got a friend. Skip Bart. He's a photographer, one of the best, and he knows the nudist business. He wouldn't charge much to locate clients for us. Besides, he owes me some for posing."

Dutch couldn't stop looking at the swollen cones of her breasts.

"Anything else?" he inquired.

"Getting set up is the main thing. You—well, yes, there is something else. If you belonged to one of the associations there'd be rules and you'd have to live up to them. I see no reason to join with anybody. Some of the camps won't take single men or girls but they'll let a man in if he's got a steady girl. In other camps if a husband wants to join and his wife won't he has to get his wife to sign a paper that it's all right. If you want to make money I see no point to any of those rules. When people want sex they're going to have it no matter what you do."

Dutch turned it over in his mind. He hadn't formed plans as to what he was going to do and if he didn't open a nudist camp somebody else would. From a moral standpoint he saw nothing wrong with it. It was an individual's own business if he or she wanted to become a sun worshiper. They wouldn't be going naked on the streets of some town. They'd be by themselves, bothering no one. And what if a guy did have his fun with some girl? She could say no, couldn't she?

"I can't lose much," he said.

"Lose? You'll win."

"What if I don't? I have to get the house and grounds in shape before I can put it up for sale. There's an old tractor in the barn and I can do the work myself, mowing the grass and like that."

"And inside the house?"

"That, too. I'm no cripple. I—Cherry, I'm sorry I said that. I didn't mean it the way it sounded. The idea was yours and if you want to throw in with me on this thing you're more than welcome. Without you or the fellow you mentioned I couldn't swing it. I've got some vague knowledge of the nudist movement but that isn't enough. Give me a power shovel on construction and I know how to use it. This camp is completely out of my line. I'd be more confused than a pig in a bag."

She moved one of her legs so that it pressed up against his. He looked down at the full line of her thigh. Strangers, he thought. Strangers met and lives changed.

"When are you leaving the city?" she wanted to know.

"Today."

"I couldn't. Not today. I'll have to see Skip and tell him."

"Is he important to you?"

"Hardly. He's just a guy with some contacts. When you operate alone you need that. Selling a nudist camp is different than selling anything else. Try knocking on doors and you'll get slammed over the head with a chair."

"But you'll follow me?"

"That's up to you, isn't it?"

"We'd be living in the same house."

"I understand that."

"And you don't mind?"

"No, because I'm not that kind of a girl."

He said nothing. She was that kind—they all were—and he'd prove it to her. If she was smart she'd resist at first but eventually he'd bend her to him. He'd explore the hills and valleys of her body with his hands, his lust rising, and she'd live as a female was meant to live. No more fooling around with a girl as he had with Penny. What did a man get out of it? He got clobbered, that's what he got for being decent. A girl was built for a man and what a girl wanted a man had for her.

Cherry Graves slid down from her stool.

"I've got to run," she said. "There's just one more appointment for me to keep."

"More nudes?"

"Yes, and this man is a creep."

"Forget him."

"I can't. I promised."

"When will I see you?"

"In a couple of days but don't meet me at the station. I can take a cab and the driver ought to be able to find the farm."

"Sure. They all know it."

She squeezed his hand briefly and walked to the door. He watched the wild sway of her hips, observed the trim, flowing lines of her legs.

"When they built her they didn't leave anything out," the bartender said after she'd gone.

"I've got a feeling that this is my lucky day."

The bartender set up a free beer.

"You know something, fellow? No day is lucky for a man when he meets a dame. I admire but I don't touch. The way I see it I'd rather have the fleas off my dog than put the blocks to any one of them."

"You've got your opinion and I have mine."

"Why not? It's a free country."

Dutch was drunk by the time he reached the railroad station.

He laughed and stumbled up the steps.

Give him a week and he'd have her.

All the way.

2

HE WORKED ALL the next morning on the tractor. Of course the battery was shot but he'd expected that. Before leaving town in a cab he'd purchased a new one, plus some oil and a five gallon can of gasoline. However, the thing was stubborn and it wasn't until now that he had it running. He wondered why he had gone to all the trouble. The grass didn't need mowing as yet and he had no other use for the machine. Yet it would be there when he had to put it into service. Anyway a man had to start somewhere.

The house was in fair condition, not counting the dust, but the lights weren't on, there was no water or a telephone. Not only that, he didn't have any food because the grocery stores had closed before the arrival of his train. It was nine miles to Cramston and he had no way of getting there without a cab.

He washed down at the lake and the smell of the pine trees pleased him. The lake, which covered about thirty acres, was ringed with pines and he was glad to note that the beach he had helped his father build was still in good condition. All the beach required was a new diving board and a few minor repairs to the raft that rested on the sand.

Actually, it was an ideal location for a group of nudists. No fences were necessary to hide them from public view. He owned the entire top of the mountain—his father had called it High View—and his nearest neighbors were the Comstocks about two miles away. Penny had been a Comstock prior to her marriage, the oldest of several children and they had the nearest phone that was available to him except for that shack Penny had moved into with Cliff Horton. Penny had always been a nut over using a phone and he doubted if she'd stay anywhere without one. He also doubted that he wanted to see her again.

"You're going to hate me," she had said that night.

"It depends."

"You will. Your parents died within three years of each other and I know how you've trusted me. I—Dutch, it's Cliff Horton. There was that night when you couldn't see me—remember?—and he came along with another couple in his car. He wanted a date and I saw nothing about it that I should have seen. I—well, I went. There was a bottle, maybe two, and all of us got to drinking. The stuff choked me and I didn't want it but they kept nagging me. I—yes, I got drunk. I didn't know what he was doing at first and then it was too late. He gave me his baby."

Two years, Dutch thought. Not a long period of time for some but a slice out of eternity for him. Two years out of the country, working, trying to forget. Two years of seeking out a girl for only one purpose. Fortunately, he had gone to a good place for that. Some of the girls refused sex but most of them didn't. Of course there was a penalty for a mistake. Knock one of them up and you had to pay until the kid was eighteen. There was no fooling around about that. He had been fortunate in that respect.

He was hungry and the only way he could get food was to call for a cab. He left the farm and started walking down the road.

He smelled of grease from the tractor but it didn't matter. He could smell worse than a dead fish in the sun and the store owners were only interested in how big a sale they could make. People were constantly worrying over money, chasing it. Maybe he was one of them. He had saved over ten thousand dollars while working in Iceland but he hadn't gone without in order to save. Things simply hadn't cost as much and the amount had just grown by itself. It hadn't taken a great deal to please a girl up there. One girl, from the year before, he could recall very well. The girl had been fond of eggs and since they weren't always in plentiful supply she'd asked him about getting her father some hens. He'd known a pilot, arranged to have the pilot smuggle in whatever number of chickens he could, and Dutch had slept with the girl for countless nights after that, in her own home. Even the mother had been great and she'd served him breakfast in bed, ignoring the fact that her daughter lay naked and willing beside him. The chickens had arrived all right but they hadn't lived long. This was during the summer and there was a shade of darkness about midnight. The old man had kept the chickens in an open pen and they'd climbed up onto their roosts to sleep as the sun had sunk into the Arctic. However, the half-light, half-darkness had only lasted about an hour and the chickens had been unable to cope with the short nights. They had died a few days apart thereby ending his romance with the girl.

The dirt road that led down off the mountain was in sad need of repair. He knew it would do no good to complain about it. The man in charge of the highway department had a thousand excuses as to why nothing was done with the chug holes. He wouldn't admit that he worked his crew in other sections of the township where there were more votes. Hell, no. He wouldn't be guilty of such a statement.

It was another hot day and he felt the heat not so much because of the change in climate but because he was remembering that delightful Cherry in the city, thought about her as almost any man thinks about a beautiful girl. Being a nudist with her wouldn't be too tough to follow through on. Even though the camp idea never got off the ground he'd have her up there in the mountains with him and that would be enough. It was too early to know the extent of his actual feelings for her but she had shaken him as no other girl had since Penny. He had used the other girls and while he wanted to use Cherry, too, there was something far deeper in his reactions toward her. The fact that he didn't recognize the reaction for what it was didn't surprise him. Penny had turned him hard inside and a man didn't lose that in a minute or an hour. Still, he knew he didn't want to go on working across the face of the earth as some men did. There was money in it, a great deal, but there was also the loneliness. His own youth had been happy, his parents loving and kind and what they had shared together stuck in his brain. A man, he supposed, ought to share with a woman, share his money and his life and his dreams. He had seen so many men who lived alone and they were empty shells of frustration. They gambled—something which he didn't do—drank too much and slept with any female who would have them.

He had witnessed the tragedy of misguided love in Iceland. So many of the children had been fathered by men from outside of the country that he had found it difficult to believe. All of it couldn't be blamed on World War II because much of it had started before then. Ships visited the island and the men left their children behind them. However, there was seldom the stigma of being looked upon as a bastard, at least not to the extent that some kids suffered here at home. The practice of naming children may have had something to do with that. A baby didn't take the father's last name. The name used was the father's first name—in the case of a girl the term "dottir" was added, to indicate daughter, and with a boy it was simply "son." In other words it could be Johnsdottir or Johnsson and since John was a very popular name it made for confusion. He had met so many on the island with the same names that he had often wondered how they managed to get their mail.

He wiped the sweat from his forehead and walked on. He should worry about that or anything else. All he had to worry over was Cherry and whether or not she kept her word. It was very easy for a girl to decide something in a bar but just as easy for her to change her mind later on. The city was big, a sprawling giant, and if she didn't come to him he would be unable to find her unless…

Nudes.

She posed for nudes so that meant she must work out of an agency. He had read about these things and most girls who modeled had somebody to represent them. This was their assurance that they wouldn't walk into a trap as the result of following a blind ad, that the atmosphere in which they posed was conductive to a high moral standard.

Nudes.

He didn't like the idea of her posing that way but it was men who bought the pictures. It seemed almost unfair to hold the girl at fault. It was the fault of the men because without a market there wouldn't be any nudes employed.

He saw the shack where Penny lived long before he got to it. Coming up through the darkness it had been merely a blot on the landscape but he noticed that it hadn't changed much or improved. The boards were still weatherbeaten, just rough boards with slats over the cracks. Nobody had lived in it for a long time before Penny and Cliff moved in but some of the wild kids had come out from town and held parties there. They'd had the booze and sex and nobody had bothered them.

As he neared the shack he noticed that white curtains were hung at the windows and that the lawn was neat and level. His steps increased. If she was home he didn't want to see her. She had stabbed him in the guts two years previously and some of the pain remained. He expected that it always would. Somehow a girl could bring more pain to a man than a bullet fired from a gun.

Just as he was opposite the shack she came around the side of the little building from the rear. His feet became clumsy and he sucked in his breath, the air burning his throat and leaving it dry. She wore red shorts and a red halter and she was more lovely than ever. Her full breasts challenged the halter and she was flat in the stomach. Her hips hadn't grown large because of the child and the material of the shorts strained upward and cut into her thighs. Her hair was a trifle longer than it had been the last time he'd seen her but the sand washed blondness was there, held back away from her ears by a red ribbon. Her face was still soft and beautiful but there was a sadness about it, too, a sadness which even her wide blue eyes and naturally red lips couldn't conceal.

"Dutch!" she screamed and rushed to him.

She slammed into his chest, her arms going around him, but he just stood there, doing nothing. She choked on her sobs and it made him feel unhappy. Married but it probably wasn't good for her. Cliff had always been wild, had never amounted to much. Handsome in a somewhat rugged way but that was all. Handsome and a heavy drinker, inclined to take anything that wasn't bolted down. That kind didn't finish out their contracts on a foreign job. Somebody took care of them and they washed out, losing everything, generally forced to pay their own fare home.

"Hey," he said gently in spite of his bitterness.

"Cut it out, will you?"

She hugged him again and then pulled away. There were tears in her eyes and on her cheeks.

"Nobody knew you were coming home, Dutch!"

"Why should I tell anybody? I didn't ask anybody when I went."

She looked up at him and smiled.

"Well, it's wonderful to see you."

"Same here." Meeting her again was torture. They had enjoyed so much that was decent together and she had traded it all for one night in a parked car by being drunk and careless. "It seems like five years," he added.

"Or longer."

"Maybe."

"When did you get in?"

"Last night."

"And you're walking."

"Sure. I haven't had a chance to pick up a car. I thought your people would let me use the phone. I don't know how they feel about things but it isn't too much to ask. If they won't let me put in a call I'll just keep on walking."

"I've got a phone."

"Thanks, but I'll stop off and see them."

"Why go that far?"

He hunted for cigarettes but he didn't have any. As he hunted he studied the peaks of her breasts and that one afternoon returned to him. They had gone swimming in the lake, just the two of them, and she'd lost the top part of the suit. She'd come out of the water, unaware at first about what had happened, and the treasures she revealed had almost knocked his eyes out of his head. Her breasts had been generous and, tilted, their dark centers sleeping. She had discovered her misfortune and snatched up a towel, laughed some, and raced for home. In another moment he would have had her before Cliff.

"You're married," he replied. "Husbands get sore when an old romance turns up out of the past. I want no part of that."

She looked down at her feet, moved one of them so that the toe of the sneaker dug a hole into the dirt.

"I guess you didn't get any news from home," she said.

"Only my deposit statements from the bank. There was no reason for me to write to anybody or for them to write to me."

"How could they write when they didn't know your address?"

"You've got a point."

"I tried the bank on a guess but they wouldn't give it to me and I had no way of finding out what company you were working for."

"You're married," he repeated. "You bought what you got and you married Cliff. A wife doesn't write to another man."

She glanced up from the hole she'd dug into the dirt.

"I'm no longer married," she said.

Thoughtfully, he ran his fingers through his hair. It figured. Cliff hadn't finished school and he had a habit of quitting on things. He'd had more jobs in a few years than any ten men.

"Well," Dutch said. "Well, how about that?"

"So you can use the phone." His question didn't require an answer. "There's nobody here except me and I doubt if my people are home anyway. Pa got called for some kind of special jury duty and Ma takes the kids down to her sisters during the day. It's about the only time they can go to the movies and it's cheaper in the afternoon. When the rest of the kids were younger Pa got along but now that they're older and they need more things it's tough. I help them all I can but even that isn't enough."

"This heat is getting me," he said. "And since you aren't married I guess there's no harm in using your phone."

"You may have to wait. They go crazy on the party line."

They crossed the lawn to the shack. Once her arm touched his and his spine crawled. She was a woman and he was a man and some of the married women were better than the others. What he was thinking of regarding her had nothing to do with love. She had buried that for him and as soon as feelings were buried they ceased to live. Love didn't have the traditional nine lives of a cat. It had one life.

He was amazed when he entered the shack. It was small with just a living room, bedroom, kitchen and bath but there was colorful wallpaper on the walls and the paint was fresh. Nobody could say the furniture was new, yet it was in good condition and attractive. She even had a television set with a full size screen. He noticed a photograph on top of the television set. It was of him, taken with his first deer.

"Some improvement," he said and crossed to the phone.

"I did it myself."

He tried the phone but somebody else was already on the line. He replaced the phone and sat down in a comfortable chair.

"Would you care for a beer?" she asked.

He laughed. If she was willing he didn't care whether or not he got into town. He'd give her what he should have given her before.

"Yeah," he said. "Yeah, I'll take a beer. I was only trying to get a cab."

"You don't need any cab. My car is in back of the shack and you can use that."

"You've got a car?"

"Naturally. How else would I go to work?"

"Work? Where?"

"In Cranston. For a lawyer. He's on a trip just now but he pays me the same as though I was working."

He helped himself to a cigarette while she was getting the beer and inhaled deeply of the smoke. It was a menthol brand, not one that he liked, but it was better than nothing.

The beer was cold but the menthol in the cigarette spoiled the taste of it. She sat on the sofa, one leg over the side and the other stretched out straight.

"Funny for you to live here when you work in town," he said.

"Maybe this is where I belong."

"But this shack—"

"Isn't it nice in here?"

"Sure. Swell."

"All right. I did the inside first so I could enjoy it. Last week I arranged for a new roof and to have shingles put over the boards. When I get done you won't know the place and it'll be mine."

He crushed out the cigarette, wished that he could taste more of the beer and less of the menthol.

"When were you divorced?" he wanted to know.

The sadness in her face became more pronounced.

"There wasn't any divorce, Dutch."

He leaned forward, looking at Penny.

"Why lie to me?" he demanded. "If you aren't divorced you're still married." He realized something was missing in the shack. "There's also the kid—"

"Please. It's what I wanted to write to you about."

"I understand." He didn't.

She shook her head.

"It was a horrible marriage, Dutch. He married me because I made him do it, because it was only right, but he got to thinking that the baby was yours and not his. I tried to reason with him. It was hopeless. He knew he was first with me but he said I'd been with you after that. He worked off and on and we nearly starved. Whenever he got any money he didn't come home."

"You couldn't miss having it rugged with him," Dutch said.

"We didn't have any hospitalization insurance. The baby was coming, and I went to work. I worked until the eighth month and then the doctor said I had to stop. I was awfully large and uncomfortable and not one word of sympathy came from Cliff. He didn't even come to the hospital when the baby was born and I needed him terribly. I was in labor for hours and the birth was difficult. I prayed that the baby would look like you, even though it wasn't yours, but the little boy was the image of Cliff."

"That should have set his thinking straight."

"It did—for a while. He got a steady job but most of it was for our son and none for me. He wanted only one thing from me and I wouldn't let him have it. I hated him but I thought for the sake of the baby I had to make our marriage work. My mother took care of the baby during the day and I got this job in the lawyer's office. Nights Cliff would come home until I put the baby to bed and then he'd go out again. He'd return, drunk and cursing, and sometimes he'd hit me."

"You should have left him."

"I know but I was trying to keep us together. I didn't love him—I hated him—but he was the boy's father and a boy needs a father. Then I made a mistake. There was extra work at the office and I worked a couple of nights a week, rather late. Somehow Cliff got the idea that the lawyer was having from me what I refused to give to him. There was no truth to it and we fought awfully.

Every night until—"

"Yes. Go on."

She said nothing more until she got fresh beer for them. This time she sat on the sofa facing him. The shorts were higher than ever on her thighs, her halter a little loose. He refused to look at the misery in her face but he did look at her body. Any man who found her would find his pleasure.

"It was on a Saturday night," she said. "I worked that day and he drew his pay at noon. By the time he came in at night he was roaring drunk. He said I was a whore, that he wasn't going to live with me and be responsible for any bastard that I might have. He said he had a woman who would care for his son and that he was getting out with the boy. I begged him to go to bed. He was too drunk to drive or to think straight. He cursed and struck me. I was helpless to stop him and he took the baby out to the car and—well, I never saw either one of them alive after that. He tried to pass a truck on the highway but he lost control of the car, knocked down a dozen posts and went over a bank. They were both dead long before anybody got to them."

"The hell," Dutch said with feeling. "What a lousy, rotten break."

"It was horrible," she admitted. "What happened to Cliff was his own fault—I couldn't even cry for him at the funeral—but the baby, so innocent and small, didn't deserve to die. It took me weeks to accept the truth but I came to the conclusion that you can't live in the past. The scars stay but you've got your life ahead of you."

"The hell," Dutch said again.

"That's why I wanted to write to you. It wasn't only that I wanted to tell you about them dying but I hoped I could make you realize that the part of me that belonged to you never once belonged to Cliff. I hoped you'd forgive me but I didn't really expect that you would. I was foolish that one night and I've paid for it. I've paid just about all a woman can pay."

"When was this?" Dutch inquired.

"Last year."

"Insurance?"

"Cliff's parents had a small policy on him but there was none on the baby. His people were fair and while they wanted to help me with the expenses for the baby I took care of that myself."

Dutch frowned. All of this should alter things but it didn't. His bitterness remained and the hardness was like a rock inside of him. She was the same as the others, to be enjoyed if she would permit him to possess her. The events of more than two years stood between them and that mattered. She'd gotten drunk with him a couple of times and once he'd had her almost naked to the waist. But he'd respected her—and it hadn't been worth it. A guy dated a girl, honored her chastity, and some slob ran the bases with her.

"You haven't lost any of your beauty," he said.

"Are you mad at me?"

"No, I'm not mad. Sorry that you found it rugged going but not mad."

She left for the kitchen and came back with more cold beer.

"I suppose you'll be going away again," she said.

"I doubt it."

"Then you're starting up the farm?" She sounded pleased.

"I've got some plans but they don't include farming."

"I guess you know your own business."

"Here's hoping."

She was silent for a moment. Much of the sadness had left her face.

"Can I be honest with you, Dutch?"

"Of course."

"It should have been you that night and not him."

"Well, it wasn't. The alarm went off and he was the first one to get to the fire."

"Please, Dutch. There were times when I wanted you that way but you didn't know it. I couldn't tell you because it's up to the man, isn't it? I mean, a girl doesn't come right out and ask."

She was wrong. Some of them did. Some of them asked and many more of them made it obvious that they wouldn't refuse.

"It's okay," he said.

The tip of her tongue found her lips.

"What's left for us, Dutch?"

"It depends on what you want."

"I've dreamed of you. Some nights I wake up and all I long for is to have you in there with me. You can call it love or sex or anything else that you wish. Before the baby was born I gave Cliff his rights but he was a drunken, brutal pig and it was never good for me with him."

Nothing was right about it, because Dutch was thinking about Cherry in the city, but he either had to have Penny or somebody else. He got that way once in a while. When he did he wasn't particular who the girl was as long as he satisfied himself.

"You've got a shape," he said to her.

"I didn't think I'd ever get it back."

"That bad, huh?"

"Only because I was ashamed of what I had inside of me, hating both Cliff and myself. Just once and he did that to me. It was difficult to believe."

"Once is all it takes."

He got the next round of beer for them and he sat with her on the sofa.

"It's hot in here," he said.

"How hot?" She was teasing him.

"Hot enough so that you don't need that halter on."

"You saw me before."

"Yeah, but not today and I've got a poor memory."

She hung onto her glass for a second when he tried to take it from her.

"What we do has to mean something, Dutch."

"Maybe it will."

He put their glasses on the floor. She came into his arms willingly and she felt good as he brought her in tight. His mouth crushed her lips in a wave of fury and he unfastened the halter. She laughed against his kiss, teasing him some more, as he pushed one hand between them and found what he wanted. She stiffened as he hurt her, then her lips parted and she relaxed.

"You have to be sure," she whispered and let her feverish mouth wander over his face.

"Who cares?" He was desperate, anxious.

"You would if I—"

"Stop worrying. Cripes!"

He got up, lifting her, and carried her into the bedroom. Twin beds, probably because of Cliff. He hated the things. A guy didn't know what he was doing at a time like this and he could break an arm if he fell off of one just right.

She gave him a look of longing after he placed her on the bed, smiling her love as she fought her way out of the shorts.

Dutch tore at his own clothing and threw the things in a pile on the floor. He told himself that he had this coming to him, that it was an old debt that he'd treated her square and she'd let some other fellow give her a kid.

He stood over her, looking down, seeing the waiting flesh that was his to have and to know.

"Dutch," she said softly, begging. "Dutch, you think—"

He went down there for her, feeling the warmth of her body, the urgency of her lips under his mouth, sensing a need that was beyond either one of them to deny.

She cried out as he took her, causing her pain. He owned her as though he was an escaped beast from the jungle, made her moan and gasp in an effort to breathe.

He didn't get to Cranston that day.

Or back home that night.

What man could be bothered with such minor details when he was so busy?

Find that man and he was already dead.

3

THE FORD WAS seven years old, a station wagon, but it was good enough for Dutch. In fact, almost anything was good enough for that mountain road.

"There's no guarantee on it," the dealer told him. "Not a month or a day."

"Who asked you for one?"

"Nobody but a lot of people get some pretty queer notions. I should guarantee another man's headache?"

However, the dealer was helpful. He arranged for a license on the wagon and the liability insurance.

Dutch had a little trouble driving over to the railroad station. In Iceland you drove on the left side of the road but here you didn't. Get over on the left side and you were ready for a casket.

He was early for the train and he stopped off at a bar for a beer. She had said for him not to meet her but he was getting impatient. Three days and she hadn't shown yet. Probably she wouldn't. Either she was busy or she had returned to Pennsylvania. No matter what it was it left him hanging from a limb.

"Beer," he told the bartender.

He hunched his shoulders and sat down on a stool. Of course he'd kept himself occupied physically but he hadn't gotten much done at the farm. He couldn't go to bed with Penny and accomplished anything else except the work that shoved them into the bed. Afterward, she always felt guilty and talked of love but for his part he was simply degrading her because of what she had done to him.

"Maybe I'll have one," she had said that morning.

"Have what?"

"Another baby. Yours."

"And maybe you won't."

The possibility annoyed him and he didn't think he would visit her again. He'd had his revenge and she was too serious. If Cherry didn't arrive from the city he'd go down there and search for her. The police were able to locate a criminal so why couldn't a man find a girl? Yet—

Strange, wasn't it? The hardness inside of him melted whenever he thought about her. A few casual drinks, those dark eyes, her black hair, her exciting body that she placed naked before a camera and she became a child of desire.

He had another beer and listened to a couple of women talking a few stools away from him.

"I don't feel sorry for you," the one woman said. "Go the limit, be stupid, and you get yourself a present that cries after nine months."

"But this will make six for us."

"Ever try sleeping alone?"

"It's a good suggestion."

He finished his drink and left the bar, waited for a couple of cars to pass and then crossed the street to the railroad station. The station didn't amount to a great deal but the same could be claimed for the rest of Cranston. It was a backward town, a quiet town that sought little from the rest of the world in the way of progress. Once it had been a large railroad center but the merchants had complained about the smoke from the old coal burning engines and the repair shops had moved out. Now there was no longer any shops, no smoke from the new diesel engines and since a merger with another railroad Cranston was an unimportant stop with an equally unimportant future.

The man at the ticket window told him the train was late but that wasn't unusual. A man could miss a date with death if he depended on the schedule published by the railroad.

It was another hot day outside and he stood in the shade of the building. A couple of retired railroad workers with nothing better to do were checking their watches, comparing past experiences and bitching about how the line had gone to pot.

"When they merged it was with the devil," the man who appeared to be the oldest said.

"Yes, but what could they do? Look at the trucks. The public pays for the highways and they ride them cheap. You can't move freight cars when there isn't any freight. And the busses and cars, they got the passenger trade."

"That's true. The railroads pay taxes on every foot of their lines but when they need help nobody ever heard of them before."

"The government has helped some."

"Well, I didn't know that."

"You do now."

Dutch yawned. The only thing he wanted from the railroad was for this next train to bring Cherry Graves to Cranston. Cherry Graves. She was some female, the best he'd ever met. She could dig a grave for herself and he'd get into it with her.

He yawned again and shook his head. That was a morbid thought. A man didn't consider the possibility of such a beautiful creature growing old or dying. In his mind she was much different than Penny. He liked Penny for what she was, for what he could take from her, but the old love which he had once felt wouldn't burn, wouldn't give off a single spark. She gave of herself without reservation, almost an animal in the final moments of physical excitement, but he couldn't believe in the love which she claimed she had for him. He decided she was simply looking for a husband, or money, or any of the other number of things for which a woman might trade her flesh.

He lit a cigarette as the train came up the track. It wasn't much of a train, just a mail car, a freight car that had been misplaced, and two passenger coaches. When he had been young the trains coming through the town had been long ones, hauling from the city westward. Now the company merely went through the motions.

The train stopped and the first person who got off was an old man with a cane. It was strange that he should have a cane. He didn't use it when he walked and he didn't limp. Maybe some people were nuts.

And then he saw her.

Cripes, she looked good. Perfect legs under sheer nylons, a red dress that struggled to conceal her curves, a waist that was pulled in with a narrow belt. Her breasts leaped forward, assaulting the material as, smiling, she swayed toward him.

He stayed right where he was.

There was a guy with her, a young man of rather average height and weight. Somewhere he had seen that thin face before but he couldn't remember the circumstances surrounding their meeting. Perhaps he had been drinking at the time. That was the bad thing about drinking—even a little bit of it clouded your brain.

"You didn't have to meet me," she said but she sounded pleased that he had.

"It was a gamble that you'd be on the train. Sometimes you gamble and you win."

The fellow with her was loaded down with a couple of suitcases. He also had a camera slung over one shoulder.

"Dutch, this is Skip," she said. "The guy I told you about. Skip Bart."

Dutch nodded but he didn't say anything. He usually formed quick impressions but he found this difficult to do with Skip. Skip's pale eyes didn't look honest although his face did.

"You've forgotten me," Skip said. "Haven't you?"

"I'm afraid I have."

"Does Sam's Bar mean anything to you?"

"Not in the least."

"We had a few drinks together."

"Did we? Well, maybe."

"You'd just gotten back into the country and you said you were coming up here to the farm. You went to the john but further down the bar you ran into some girl. You left with her."

Dutch grinned. It could be true all right. He'd torn into the booze as soon as he'd gotten off the plane and much of that first night was shrouded in mystery.

"I was drunk," he said for Cherry's benefit. "She was a tramp and I didn't know what I was doing. I only know I gave her money for nothing."

Cherry laughed.

"You don't have to apologize," she said. "That's your business and none of mine."

Dutch took one of the suitcases and they walked around the station and over to the Ford. Cherry said she thought he'd be driving a new car but he asked her why he should waste all that extra money wasn't necessary.

"No reason," she said as she sat between them. "Only when a fellow returns home he usually blows his change."

"Not me."

"I guess you're wondering about me," Skip said as Dutch pulled away from the curb.

"A little. There's nothing up here for you."

"This nudist thing has to go over or there's no point to it, is there?"

"Hardly."

"So I talk to people about coming and most of them want to see pictures of the place."

"Now I get it."

"Not so much with the girls but with the man. With the men I have to show them pictures of some of the girls, too. These guys are out for a holiday and the more flesh you can offer the higher the price you get. Fortunately, I've got the girls and they're no problem—plenty of nude studies to pass around. Hunting down the men is no easy job but I'm not a cripple."

"This sounds more like sex for sale than a nudist camp," Dutch decided. "Like weigh up fish at a meat counter. Pay the charge and you take the fish with you."

"Don't be silly," Cherry said. "If everybody ran around naked there wouldn't be near the interest in sex that there is. That's the way it is at a nudist camp. The people take their nude bodies for granted but it's better if the girls are pretty rather than ugly. I won't deny that things do happen at a camp but they happen all over the country anyway. If people are going to do wrong they don't have to be nudists to throw gasoline onto a fire that's already there."

Dutch wiped the sweat from his forehead. She was close to him, smelling clean and wonderful, and he felt the nagging fire inside, the ancient fire of the male that wanted the female. He longed for her as a hungry man longs for food, a thirsty man for water. He wanted her as he'd had Penny, willing and responsive, naked and yielding, but there was no other relationship between the two wants. He had degraded Penny with his body, used her for his own satisfaction, taken what she had given to another man in folly. With Cherry his desires, trapped and bitter for the past two years, went beyond that. Of course he didn't know her well enough to understand the depth of his feelings but she had bored through the surface and she was into his blood.

"They told me there was a bus for the city about nine tonight," Skip said.

"I guess there used to be one."

"Swell. I'll take a few pictures and catch that. My money is made in the city. Up here in the sticks I'd starve to death."

He was glad the photographer wasn't staying.

"What am I going to owe you?" he asked.

"Owe me? Nothing. I charge the men for my tip on the camp and I get my pay from that. Then when you open I'll work the grounds and get a few nude studies to sell. It's no way of becoming rich but I make out. Click a camera for a living and die poor. So what?"

"Thanks for your help," Dutch said.

They were both impressed with the farm when they reached it.

"Perfect," Cherry said as she got out. "A big house, some other buildings, a large barn, plenty of grass and that lake. Skip, you could promote a scene like this in the dark."

"Yeah. I'll get my snaps and work them up."

Skip wandered off and Cherry wanted to be shown everything.

"The barn first," he told her.

The barn had once housed cows by a former owner but his father had had all of the equipment torn out, selling it to raise money for seed and the expense of plowing. For a building so old it was in good shape, the walls inside painted white.

"You could set up cots in here," she said. "You can buy them surplus and they're cheap."

"What about privacy?"

"All you have to do is hang up some sheets. When I mentioned privacy I meant from outsiders. You've got that here and there isn't much privacy in a nudist camp. Anybody whose ashamed of their body wouldn't come here in the first place."

She thought a small shed off the barn which had once been used as a milk cooling room would make a fine snack stand. This, she claimed, he almost had to have and it would bring in extra income. As for working it they could take turns and, she added, one of the guests might want to make a few bucks by helping out.

Everything appealed to her, especially the interior of the house.

"It needs cleaning but with seven bedrooms you can haul in a fortune. A few couples will want to be alone and you can clip them plenty for that."

"Married couples, huh?"

Her eyes smiled up into his face.

"Who cares about that? Married or single they all do the same thing when they're together."

"I suppose they do."

"We have no control over their morals."

"How could you control a man with a lot of naked girls about?"

"I doubt if it's as tempting as you think."

"You have to prove that to me."

"Maybe I will." She laughed. "And sooner than you expect."

The power company had turned the current on and he got some beer from the refrigerator. They sat at the kitchen table, drinking the beer and waiting for Skip. She was across from him, her breasts high and ripe and he knew that he'd never be able to endure the pressure if he saw her stripped naked. He'd take her with savage force, crush her body violently, beautifully.

"We'll scrub and clean like a couple of fools," she said.

"I could hire somebody."

"Why do that? If you hired somebody they'd stick their nose into your affairs and the quieter we keep this operation the better it will be for us."

"Then we are violating the law?"

"Oh, no. Not in this state. It's legal and as long as the members who come here pay their dues, leave other folks alone it's all right. We just don't want a lot of curious prowlers out for a cheap thrill."

"I understand."

Skip came in and he had a beer with them. He said he liked scotch better but that he drank beer mostly.

"I make plenty of money but I have a habit of betting on the wrong horses," he explained. "Therefore I wind up with beer instead of scotch. It doesn't matter too much. It all goes the same place and you can get just as drunk on one as you can the other." He smiled at Dutch. "I ought to hate you for stealing my best model."

"I think she was getting tired of it anyway," Dutch said.

"If there are truer words I never heard them," Cherry agreed. She glanced at Skip. "I didn't mind it with you because you keep your mind where it belongs but some of the others just can't tell you to change your position. They have to paw you and it makes you feel dirty. I believe that several of them hired a model mainly due to an urge to see a naked female. Certainly some of the poses were too daring for commercial use. I'd rather be up here in the hills than go through that again."

"You get that kind," Skip said. "Burt, on the other hand, many of the girls ask for it. They don't care what they do as long as they're paid."

It was dark when Dutch left the house to drive Skip Bart to the bus terminal. Cherry declined to ride along because she wanted to put her clothes away and find a place to sleep. Dutch could have told her where he wanted her to sleep but he knew it was too soon for that.

"Has Cherry worked for you long?" he asked Skip as they bumped over the road.

"About two years."

"No trouble selling her pictures?"

"None in the least until recently but now I'd say her market was fading. That has nothing to do with her body. She's got enough curves for two girls but the average male is as fickle as the weather. They not only want a new shape but a new face to go with it. Dozens of girls drift in the nude field in the hopes of drawing attention to themselves but there is little in it for them except an uncertain living."

"Most of them are tramps, aren't they?"

"A few but a tramp is far more rare than common. Most of the girls are decent and innocent when they enter the racket. I won't lie about some of them changing because they do. They've got good figures and they use them. A hundred bucks a night is big money and they fall into the gutter."

"What about the girls you'll be sending up here?"

"Most of them don't have to be asked twice."

"Is that a healthy situation?"

"Why concern yourself with it? If a girl does something with a man that's her business."

It looked like an explosive arrangement to Dutch but he didn't argue the point. He hadn't gone through with the idea yet and he might not. The fact that he had Cherry up in the house was enough for him. And the fact that he hadn't as yet had Cherry as a woman was frustrating.

"I'll be in touch," Skip said when he got off at the bus station.

Dutch didn't wait for the arrival of the bus but turned around and began driving toward the farm. He drove slowly, thinking. Things seemed to be all right—and they didn't. It was the same as trying to put a puzzle together, feeling that it was easy and then discovering that several pieces were missing. He had been drinking heavily that night, perhaps had talked to Skip Bart more than he should and the next day he had met Cherry. It seemed odd that these two should be associated and yet he supposed it could be added up as being a matter of pure luck.

As he approached Penny's shack he slowed the car even more. He could go in there and get what he needed, please himself and satisfy the past when he hurled her to the bed and took her.

Yes, there was nothing to it.

But he didn't turn in at her lane.

Promise awaited him at the top of the mountain.

Maybe…

4

THE MAN IN the store knew him. Since his return to Cranston he had been in for beer and his parents had traded there for a number of years. It was a privately owned store and while it had a complete stock of almost everything the man never made a great deal of money. He had too many charge accounts and half of the people didn't pay him.

"Must be going to do some cleaning," he said when Dutch pushed the carriage up to the register.

"That's what I was told to get."

"You were told right. It's good stuff."

"So is the beer."

"Yes, a man has to have that."

He paid for his purchases and carried the box out to the car. It was early in the morning, not yet nine, and there was hardly anybody on the street. Those who had jobs were already at work and the housewives had duties to perform around their homes.

He groaned as he got in behind the wheel. They'd gone to bed late the night before and the only thing he'd gotten from Cherry was a list of what they needed from the store. Sleep had been impossible as he'd tossed on the bed, thinking about her down the hall, the animal in him not wanting to spend the night alone. Twice he had started for her room and twice he had returned to his own bed to eventually go to sleep and dream of human flesh.

Her flesh.

The flesh of female fury.

The fury of desire and submission.

He gave the Ford plenty of power going out of town. It rattled but it could move and he was in a hurry. She hadn't been up when he'd left the house and he craved to see her. They'd be together, drink together, work together and at the proper moment she would belong to him.

Penny was in front of her shack doing something with a flower garden and although she waved at him he didn't stop. He returned the wave and plowed up the mountain.

Cherry was seated at the kitchen table when he arrived. She had made coffee and she wore a blue robe that was just about as thin as one of the curtains in the living room. He placed the box on a chair, put the beer away and poured a cup of coffee for himself.

"Now the work starts," he said and joined her at the table.

"It won't be so bad. This is a big house but you can do a lot if you stick at the job."

"Sorry. I meant to get you a bottle of liquor but I forgot."

"Beer is all right."

"It'll make you fat."

"A little of it won't."

He stirred his coffee.

"Aren't you lonely up here?"

"Nobody gets lonely if they make up their mind they won't be."

Dutch lit a cigarette.

"Where do we start?"

"My suggestion is to do the upstairs first. If we don't wouldn't we get all of that dust down here?"

"I don't know."

She was thoughtful for a moment.

"What do you think of Skip?" she asked.

"Is it important?"

"Not very."

"Well, I don't know about him either. I suppose there are all sorts of ways of making a living. I doubt if I would want his. I'm not even sure that I like him being in on this. That's honest, Cherry. He could be bad news in a rather huge manner."

"He doesn't take chances."

"In his field he must."

"Maybe but he's clever. And what would we do without him? He has the contracts and we don't. With what we have to offer we couldn't join an organization. These nudist groups are careful and they inspect your camp, not only before the season but during it."

"I'm going to feel funny," he said.

"Funny? Why?"

"Running around naked. Or can I wear my clothes?"

"No, you have to be nude. Shoes or sneaks are all right and so is a hat but count the rest out. You almost need a hat so you can carry cigarettes and matches under it. Most camps prohibit dancing unless the dancers are dressed but we don't have to worry about that. Can you imagine doing the Twist in the raw?"

"Barely, and that's not a pun. If the girl was pretty I don't see how a man could ever get through a dance."

He got more coffee for them but she didn't seem interested in hers.

"You're going to get used to being a nudist," she told him. "You can't have the camp's owner getting worked up over every curve."

"That's a neat trick if you can do it."

She smiled.

"Dutch, it's no trick at all. We'll be naked for the summer and most nudists work that way. The best thing for you to do is to come to accept it right here in the house."

He scratched his head.

"Huh?" he inquired.

"Why don't we do our work in the nude?"

He felt his head begin to pound.

"Jeeze," he said thickly. "You want me to go insane?"

"There's nothing to it. You don't feel uncomfortable with a bunch of naked people when you're also naked. You only feel uncomfortable when you're dressed. That's why the various camps have a rule that anybody on the reservation should be stripped. Besides, you create suspicion if you aren't. A lot of important people go to these places and they have to be careful. They feel that what they do is right and moral but too many folks frown on the practice."

He carried his cup over to the sink. His knees felt weak and his hands shook as he tried the water to see if it was hot. It was. At least the heater was working.

"I guess if we're going to get anything done we'd better sail into it," he said.

"Not until we—"

She left the sentence unfinished and he swung toward her, his back to the sink.

"Yeah? Until we what?"

"Go nudist."

The pulse beat wildly at the base of his throat. He could feel the beat sweep through him, finally roaring up into his head and coming to a shattering pound between his eyes. Nude. The two of them in the house. Two people—a lush female and the male. She couldn't mean it. He must be dreaming this, just as he had dreamed about her the night before.

"Aren't you pushing your luck?" he heard himself saying.

"We have to get used to each other."

"Yeah, but—"

"What's the difference whether it's now or later?"

"You've been to nudist camps. I haven't."

"Haven't you seen a woman?"

"Naturally."

"And slept with them?"

"What man hasn't?"

"Some don't."

"They're not my type. You can place your last dollar betting on that. You can—"

"Your clothes," she said impatiently. "You've got to learn. Who knows what we do? Who gives a darn? And you won't think about me as you believe you will. Few people are as attractive with their clothes off as they are with some of it on. A girl draped in a filmy gown is more sexy than a nude."

He shrugged. This was real and that was for certain. He had nothing to lose.

Dutch was wearing a T-shirt and that came off first. He had a massive chest, powerful shoulders and a flat stomach. Air plunged down into his lungs and then came out in a rush.

"You," he said thickly. "Now."

She laughed.

"Why not?"

She stood up and unbelted the robe. She got out of it easily and dropped it over the back of one of the chairs.

He couldn't think clearly and it was almost impossible for him to breathe. His lungs fought for air and the pound between his eyes grew steadily worse.

She was all that he imagined her to be — and more. Her breasts were swollen mounds of delight, gently curved beneath and rising upward, thrusting out. They were rich of all that was woman and down below her skin was smooth, her curves maddening.

A flower, he thought.

A flower to be plucked and kept.

"Go on," she coaxed.

"Aw, hell, I—"

"Of course it's a shock but it'll wear off. In less than an hour I'll be just another person, nobody special. You don't do this for the purpose of sex. You do it so you can enjoy yourself, so that you can be free. What are clothes for anyway? I'll tell you what they're for. The phonies hide inside of them."

With fumbling hands he undressed, then stood naked before her. He searched her eyes for some reaction but if there was any he couldn't find it. Maybe, he decided, there was something to what she had said. Maybe being nude had nothing to do with the emotions that guided and brought about physical love.

"Don't you feel more at ease?" she asked.

"Are you kidding? I don't know how I feel. Getting undressed with a girl before never had but one ending. It wasn't true of the girls in Iceland but I couldn't accept that completely. I doubt if any man from this country could."

She crossed over to the box.

"Get some water in a bucket," she said.

"The bucket's outside."

"Then get it."

"I'm not dressed."

Her smile flashed.

"Stop being so much aware of yourself, Dutch. I'm sure I'm not, except that you're a big, strong man. Most men are alike and so are most girls. There may be a little more fat here and there, a difference in curves or muscle tone, but the basic individual is pretty much the same."

He dashed out onto the porch and grabbed up the bucket. It seemed almost indecent to go out there that way but he supposed a man could become accustomed to just about anything.

They worked together that morning, in the same room. He lived and died through hell, and died again. She was a good worker and she accomplished more than he did. However, there was no complaint on her part because she seemed to understand his inner turmoil.

"This is the weirdest thing I've ever done," he said once.

"Pay attention to what you're doing. You're leaving streaks on the paint."

He glanced toward the bed.

"I know what I'd like to be doing."

"Oh, shut up." But she wasn't angry.

"There may be some value to all of this," he said another time. "At least a guy who's a nudist knows what he's getting."

"So does the girl."

"You've got plenty to get."

"Won't you please shut up?"

They had soup for lunch, which was the quickest thing to fix, and he stared at her across the table. She appeared to be unperturbed by her lack of covering and she returned his frank appraisal with one of her own that was equally frank.

"You men are all alike," she said.

"Are we?"

"Of course. A girl has to have a shape or you don't want her. You don't look past the skin and into the heart. You only wonder if she will refuse or consent. If she refuses you don't want to have anything more to do with her. If she consents she isn't any good, has no decency and you don't want to have nothing to do with her either, except for your own pleasure. She drifts from man to man and she never gains a foot of ground. What happens to her? All the way from getting pregnant to killing herself."

He found a cigarette on top of the table.

"Cut the speech," he said. "This isn't a one-way street. There's a girl and a guy and they get together. So he rocks her and she rocks him. Don't tell me she isn't just as anxious as he is. I'll buy that the second Tuesday of next week. If a girl wouldn't a guy couldn't."

"Yes, that's true enough but very often a girl doesn't have much choice."

"That's one side of it." He didn't like the soup. "How about a beer?"

She shook her head.

"That's not very smart the way we are."

"Why?"

"Because we all have certain barriers that we place between ourselves and others and drinking only tears them down. I didn't come up here to amuse you in bed or to go back to the city with your child inside of me. I came to make some money and to help you make it."

"Is that the only reason."

She glanced away from him.

"Well, I like you, Dutch. You're a man and I've seen too many who weren't. They pad their shoulders, the way a woman uses falsies, and they think they're big shots. They make ten or fifteen thousand a year but they wouldn't have enough to crawl out of the water if they fell in. Back home the men were entirely different. They drank and brawled and they either won or they lost. I—well, there was a fellow once. He wasn't too tall but he was rugged and I think he loved me. The trouble was there couldn't have been any future in marriage to him. When a girl marries she has to think of any children she may have, how the father can provide for them. You can't imagine what they've done to the coal region. People use gas or oil and those who live there know only one way of making a living. Now most of that is gone, or a big part of it. It's shot and thousands of futures went down the drain."

"Things can get rough," he said.

"Yes, and I don't want them rough. You go through this life once so why make it miserable for yourself? My belly crawled with hunger when I was a kid. It isn't going to crawl again."

He stubbed out the cigarette.

"This is only for the summer," he reminded her. "What are your plans then?"

"I take what I get."

He grinned. He knew what he wanted her to take all right. He wanted her to accept him in passion, without regard for the consequences.

She finally consented to a beer and they each had one. He didn't care about working and he guessed she didn't either. They had lots of time to do what needed to be done. He'd have to get a grill and arrange to keep the soda cold but he could use tubs of ice for the soda. Beer, unless the people brought it themselves, was out of the question. A license was needed for the sale of beer and he wasn't going to the bother of trying to get one.

They were still seated at the table when the kitchen door was pushed open and Penny walked inside. She started to say something, then stopped as her eyes grew wide when she saw they weren't wearing anything.

"Real nice neighbors you've got," Cherry said acidly. "Don't they ever bother to knock?"

"This is the country," Dutch said.

Penny bit down on her lower lip and glanced up at the ceiling.

"It's getting to be some country," she declared. "People sitting around in the raw." Her glance moved from the ceiling to Cherry. "She's beautiful, Dutch, but why did you lead me on?"

"Nobody led you on."

"I disagree. You did."

"All right. Have it your own way. I led you on. What did you do to me."

"I thought I was forgiven for that."

"You're not. I went with you and he got you caught."

"I told you—"

"I know what you told me but that doesn't say I believe it. You married the guy, didn't you?"

"Dutch, I've been honest about the whole thing. I married him, yes. I married him so my baby could have a father and now they're both gone."

Cherry arose from the table. She was lovely, her tremendous breasts rising and falling gently.

"This is personal," she said. "I'll get back to work."

She left the kitchen and the lure of her liquid, flowing body became an overpowering need inside of him.

"Another girl," Penny said bitterly. "I should have known. You were giving me the man in you but not your love."

"Did I say it was love? Huh? Did I lie or mislead you? No. I got what I should have had years ago."

Wearily, she sat down at the table.

"Dutch," she said. "Dutch, I'm in trouble."

"Don't blame me. I haven't been back long enough for that."

"No, not that kind of trouble. I—there's a second girl in the lawyer's office with me. She's been with him for years but he paid me more money because I did better work. I knew she was jealous but I trusted her. When he went away I had the key to the petty cash box. Since I lived out here and she offered to check on the mail every morning I gave her the key in case she needed any money. Now she called me and said the cash was short and that I must have taken it."

"A nice person not to know."

"Forget that. Do you know what it means?"

"Why not? You just tell the lawyer the truth and hope that he can spot her lie. If he trusted you before he ought to trust you now."

"With her saying that she saw me take it?"

"That's not so good," Dutch decided.

"I won't be able to get another job, will I?"

"It'll hurt you if you get fired for that. You can be accused of almost anything except stealing or rape or murder and get away with it."

"Well, she got her revenge."

"Yes, I'd say that she did. Or she will. It's a tough charge to buck."

"Tell me," she said. "Tell me, Dutch, where do I get another job?"

He thought about it. He didn't want to work the snack bar during the summer himself and he'd rather that Cherry didn't have anything to do with it. The place for her was in his bed. She'd be more than competent at that task.

"I've got something for you," he said.

"Don't be nasty."

"No. A job. At my snack bar."

"Since when did you have a snack bar?"

"I haven't got one yet but I'll build it. We—look, we're starting a nudist camp up here. We—"

"A—what?" She was shocked.

"A nudist camp for naked people."

"You're crazy."

"Maybe I am."

"The neighbors will hate you."

"Will they? Who gives a damn? I don't. They've done nothing for me and I've done nothing for them. They—"

"Dutch—"

"It's legal. A guy comes up here, finds a broad and maybe he makes her. Maybe he doesn't. I've got no interest in that."

She began to pout.

"It's fantastic. Utterly out of this world. And that girl—you don't know how I felt when I saw her here at the table. Sure, people undress together but they're in love or married. I can understand and see that. But to just—well, I don't know. For the mere sake of—Dutch, it's the most foolish thing you've ever done. And you, sitting there that way. Where is your respect?"

"Who said I ever had any?"

She shook her head sadly.

"This isn't necessary. There are jobs on the highway and you're a construction worker. The pay is good. Yet you—how do you know anybody will come here?"

"Cherry is an expert."

"The girl?" The question was almost a sneer. "Oh, no doubt she's quite expert at—"

"Knock it off. Do you hear me? Knock it off. Cripes! This is my land and I do as I please with it. We won't bother any of the neighbors as long as they leave us alone." He rubbed the hair on his chest with one huge hand. "Now let's get around to you. You won't get any work if you're fired for stealing money, whether or not you're guilty or innocent, but there are a lot of things to be done here and I'll pay you to help us. You can't just sit down there outside of your shack, dreaming and look at the sun. You've got to have the bucks today or you're flat on your fanny. The snack bar wouldn't be difficult, only hot dogs and burgers, some soda and candy. Plus cigarettes and the sun glasses and skin lotion that Cherry told me you have to have."

"I couldn't," she said.

"I'm making the offer. You can refuse it."

She drew a deep breath.

"But, Dutch—Dutch, nobody would have anything on."

"No. Including yourself."

"I—did I hear you right? Nothing on?"

"You heard straight. People wear clothes on the street so you wear them, too. Up here you're just like one of the others."

She thought about it and he felt an inward glow of satisfaction. She was trapped in some kind of a mess and he'd degrade her even more. Using her wasn't the important thing. Smashing her down, never letting her forget, was what he sought. Down there in the shack her shame had been minor because she had believed it to be love. Here on his own land she'd be a human slave and her past would meet the present and future. Not that he wanted any other man with her. For some reason he didn't. He would take her whenever the opportunity presented itself and he'd make her crawl.

"I'm going," she said.

"Go ahead. I asked you, didn't I? What more do you want?"

She walked to the door and turned.

"For you to be reasonable, Dutch. That's what I want." She blinked the tears from her eyes. "You hate me, don't you? You hate me and there isn't anything bad enough for me, no depth that is too low."

"The hell," he said.

She opened the door and swung it back and forth slowly.

"I don't blame you any. I did a terrible thing to you and I know that some people can't forgive easily—or at all. As for the girl—well, that's your business. And hers. The only claim on you is what I feel in my heart. It isn't simple for me to love or to want love, Dutch. I went through a garbage pit with Cliff and I'm still not over losing the baby. Those things mark you, no matter what you do. You get to the point where you just don't care any more. I—about that snack bar, I don't know. I have to think about doing such a thing. Maybe—oh, it isn't any worse than what I have done to myself already. Anyway it's not much worse."

"Let me know," he said.

She went out and closed the door behind her. He sat there for a few minutes, thinking. Finding them that way must have really shook her and perhaps in offering to help her he was making a mistake. Yet the mistake, if there was one, was a mistake that he wanted to make. She'd be ashamed of herself, defeated, and he'd glory in that. Or would he? He wasn't sure and that was the lousy part of it. When you tore down a house you took off the roof first. Here he was trying to pull the foundation out from under her, to collect for their nights of decency, to make her pay for her error.

Somewhat later he walked upstairs. He hadn't been anxious to work that morning and he cared less about doing so just then. Scrubbing and cleaning wasn't a man's work. A man should build and create. He grinned. Create. Yeah, that was it. Create with his mind and hands and his body. Create new life with a beautiful girl and love her always. Establish a home, get up with the kid at night, buy groceries every Saturday, the papers on Sunday and watch the wife as she got large with the second child. Not a third. Two was plenty. No, not a third unless there was an accident.

He found Cherry in the room where they had been working. The bucket stood near the middle of the floor and he should have missed stumbling over it but he didn't. He cursed as the water spilled, ran across the bare wood, probably started to leak through one of the ceilings on the first floor. She lay on the bed, smiling up at him, the mere sight of her body an electric shock that gripped every nerve center.

"Your friend go?" Cherry asked.

"Yeah."

"I guess she didn't like me."

"Who worries?"

The blonde loveliness stirred on the bed. The roots of the hair on top of his head threatened to pull loose.

"She an old flame of yours, Dutch?"

"One that went out."

"Just like the others?"

"There haven't been any others."

"That's funny."

"Is it? Get your hands burned once and you stay away from fires. Unless—"

"Yes?"

He moved closer to the bed. Her lush beauty made him ache all over and his legs felt numb, uncertain.

"Unless you find what you want."

"And then?"

"You walk through the fire."

She lifted herself up on one elbow. There was no sag to her breasts. They rose away from her body like hills on a mountain.

"I said I wasn't that kind."

"I remember."

"I'm not."

"Until it's right for you."

Her eyes were dark, searching, filled with emotion.

"Yes, Dutch," she admitted slowly. "Until it's right."

"This is right. This—"

"Is it? When does a girl know?"

"Afterward."

"Sometimes afterward is too late."

He sank down on the bed beside her.

"Tell me in an hour if it's wrong or too late." He could hardly talk. "Tell me if it's wrong between us."

"Dutch, be sensible." It was a mild suggestion, lacking all hint of protest.

He turned toward her.

"Look," he said as the warmth of her nearness made him desperate. "This may be a game with you, Cherry, but I'm not playing in left field when I should be pitching. That's pretty good, isn't it? I pitch and you catch I—just what kind of a man do you think I am? I'm human. This crazy belief that you have, that people can exist this way, may be swell but I can't accept it. With somebody else I suppose it might be possible for me to do that but not with you. I've wandered. I've seen things. I've slept with girls I couldn't even recognize the next day. But that was before and this is now. This is being here with you and needing you and wanting you so much that I don't even know my own name. It's—."

His mouth discovered her lips, the pressure of his kiss forcing her head back onto the pillow. Her lips remained impassive as her eyes bored into his, their meaning complete and honest, and then she moved her lips under his mouth. They were soft and full and wet, parting as she began to respond.

"Please!" he groaned.

His hands roamed her body as a savage roams the darkness of an unknown jungle. He filled his hands with her, sensing the rich beauty of her flesh, and he bore down on her mouth, crushing her lips. She twisted nearer to him, moaning with longing and anticipation, her restraint shattered, her fingernails clawing at his skin, bringing pain, turning the desire that he felt into raw, reckless lust.

"Don't ever make me sorry," she whispered.

"Oh, baby, I won't."

"Don't say that."

"Don't say what?"

"Baby, I—"

"What of it? To hell with it. This is today and this is when we live. This is—"

"Make me live," she moaned.

He made her live all right. She lived as a woman and as an animal, lived in his arms in a way that he had never known another girl to live.

And he lived himself.

Lived.

Wonderfully.

5

SHE BELONGED TO him night and day after that but it didn't take him long to find out that she was an expensive lover. Cherry wanted things, only the best, and he got them for her. He didn't mind and whenever he had a doubt, just a vague one, he returned to her body. In her arms any doubts that he might have had faded and became nothing.

"We could get married," he said one morning. Naked, she was standing before the mirror, combing her hair.

"Dutch, we've got everything we could possibly have in marriage."

"Sure."

"And marriage is like quicksand. You can step into it but then try to get yourself out."

"We ought to be pretty certain about each other by now." He sat up on the edge of the bed. "If we aren't we never will be."

"Is anybody ever certain?"

"Not always."

"Then why spoil it? We're good for each other the way things are. There are no ties to hold us, no regrets to face."

"You could have one very big regret," he reminded her.

"Oh, that. Well, I'm not afraid. I was the first time but I'm not any more. A girl who indulges has to expect to take her chances. As long as she trusts the man there is no need for fear."

"Tell the social drum beaters that. You'd get a slap in the mouth."

"Yes, but I don't worry about other people. I worry about us and what we can do to make the whole picture better for us. What they say doesn't effect me." She swung to face him, her lovely body glowing in all its female splendor. "Ours isn't the cheap love of the slums where it doesn't matter and it isn't the smut that you find in a hotel room. That's far from being love. That's sex for the sake of sex and what we know goes far beyond that."

He got a cigarette and lit it. He didn't know why. A cigarette never tasted very good to him the first thing in the morning. After his coffee having one was a habit but just then it seemed to be a necessity.

"I'm still plugging for marriage," Dutch said.

"For how many times and with how many girls?"

"Am I that ugly?"

"I didn't say that."

"Well, I told you, didn't I? I considered it once before."

"Yes, but it was kind of a silent understanding. Or maybe there wasn't any understanding at all."

"So she got a baby by somebody else. How sweet of her to be so considerate. You take her out and another guy mows her grass."

He got up from the bed and stretched.

"Forget it, Cherry. I piled dirt over the past. When I start digging it up again I'll shoot myself."

She came over to him and drifted into his arms.

"Maybe I couldn't stand marriage to you," she said lightly. "You never let me sleep."

He kissed her.

"Who woke who up this morning?"

She laughed and returned his kiss.

"Honey, once in a while there's an emergency."

They went down to the kitchen and she made coffee. The coffee she made was seldom very good but he didn't complain about it. When he drank the stuff without milk, getting the full strength, it wasn't so bad.

"Would you mind if I rode down to the city today?" she asked.

He shrugged. That meant more money.

"Can't you get what you want in town?"

"Where could we buy cots at surplus prices?"

"I see."

"The time to buy is when the demand isn't there. With the weather we're having we can almost count on an early season. Once people are looking for cots the price will go up."

She poured their coffee and sat down at the table. He couldn't look at her without getting an idea but it wasn't as bad as that first day. He hadn't believed that it was possible for a man to get used to a naked female, or almost used to her, but his own reactions indicated that this was true.

"We could still pull out of this deal," he said.

"That would be a stupid thing to do."

"Would it? I'm not so sure. I've got some money and I think I can sell the property. We'd buy a trailer in the beginning and follow the construction jobs. You wouldn't be able to splurge on clothes the way we have but that wouldn't hurt you any. I don't know what you want clothes for anyway. You never wear the damned things around here."

She ignored the remark.

"What about Skip?" she inquired.

"I've got no obligation to him. When the train stops he gets off."

Cherry frowned.

"You're overlooking something, Dutch. We've both got an obligation to him. He's working for us right now, getting customers, and you can't kick that out of the window."

"Now—"

"And we can use the money. No matter how much we can get together we'll always need more. Even if you had thirty thousand it wouldn't last forever. A trailer would set us back a bundle and you might not find a job right away. Why pass up what we can have?"

He quit the subject. She had her hopes built around a big season and he thought enough of her to go along with it. They'd go for broke and pick up their dimes in the fall. Then they'd shag down to Florida and hit the sand. Or a bed. They couldn't do anything on the sand.

"There's a problem about the barn," he said. "What do we do for a bathroom for the guests?"

"Isn't there water?"

"Yes. The other people had it for their cows. The line is capped but it could be opened."

"Then you put in only the essentials. If that costs too much then we can use those chemical outfits they sell."

"People have to wash."

"The majority of nudists don't need a sink because they don't use soap."

"And they're supposed to be clean?"

"It isn't that. You've got a lake and plenty of sand. Half of the soap put out doesn't help your complexion. You get wet and then you scrub yourself with sand, rinse off in the lake when you're finished."

"Now I've heard everything."

"Why? The sand doesn't irritate the skin. It makes it pink if you aren't tanned and jumps the circulation of your blood. Some of the people who come here, the majority of them, won't know about that but they can be taught."

"There's something else that jumps your circulation," Dutch said, grinning.

"I'm talking about getting clean."

"What's dirty in that?"

"Nothing if you believe in what you're doing and in the person who's with you."

They talked some about her trip and he agreed to let her use the Ford. There were other things they needed, such as skin lotions and some other stuff that couldn't be purchased locally at wholesale, and he gave her a few signed checks so she could pay for whatever she bought.

"And a printer," she added. "We need forms when people sign in. I've got one from another camp that can be duplicated."

"It's your baby."

She laughed as she arose from the table.

"Cross your fingers, Dutch. It's the only baby I want."

"Sure. What girl needs a love child?"

She hesitated.

"What if I don't get back tonight?"

"I'd worry. I'd figure you were in an accident or something."

"But there's so much to do in one day."

"I know."

"Couldn't I call that girl down the road if I'm delayed?"

"You could call her but she might not deliver the message."

"I'll risk that. Just make up your mind that she isn't going to deliver something else to you."

"I don't want what she's got."

"Maybe it'll turn out to be the same with me."

"Never."

"Promise?"

"Today and always."

She got away from the farm about ten and he put on his clothes. Being naked in the house with her was all right but he couldn't seem to bring himself to wander around outside without being covered.

He located some tools in the barn and started in on the milk room that they were going to use for a snack stand. It wasn't really difficult work but some of the wood was old and almost all that he tore off of one side couldn't be used for a counter. Within an hour he had hit so many nails with the hand saw that the teeth were almost as dull as the back of the thing. He hauled the useless lumber out of the way and then went up to sit on the steps of the back porch.

The sun was hot and he had a cigarette. In the beginning he hadn't thought there was too much work to do but within the past couple of days he'd changed his mind. It wasn't that the job was tremendous but simply that they hadn't gotten at it. He studied the end of the cigarette. Well, if he hadn't gotten at the job he'd certainly gotten at Cherry. He'd gotten at her the way a man wanted to get at a woman, exhausted himself with her body.

He was still sitting on the steps when he heard a car and seconds later he saw a Caddy pull in and stop. Only a few people in town owned a Caddy and he didn't expect to see one up there on the mountain. Still, his father had sold fishing permits for the lake at one time and maybe somebody thought he was doing the same thing. If that was the case the man was out of luck. The man didn't have a boat and there were none on the farm. Dutch was having a few built in town for the nudists but they wouldn't be completed to the end of the week.

The man who got out of the car was fat and short. He had a red face, also fat, and he wore a suit that had probably cost three times what it was worth.

"Is this High View?" the man asked.

"People have called it that."

"Well, is it?"

"Yeah, it's High View. I don't know of another one."

The man squinted into the sun.

"That your lake down there?"

"It's no mirror."

"Friendly, aren't you?"

"Maybe not but you're a stranger."

"You won't get much business with that attitude."

"So? There's no fishing."

The man stared at Dutch.

"Who cares about fishing? I only wanted to see your place."

"It isn't for sale."

"Who said I was buying?"

"Nobody. One guess is as good as another."

The man unbuttoned his coat.

"You must know Skip Bart."

"Sure."

"He sent me."

"Now I get it. You're—"

"It doesn't matter who I am. I wanted a week away from things and he seemed to have a pretty good proposition. I pay my money and I get what I'm after." He glanced around. "You've got rooms in the house?"

"Yes, there are rooms."

"How much for a week?"

"I couldn't tell you. We haven't set any rates yet."

The man wiped the sweat from his face with a handkerchief.

"That's not important," he said. "As long as it's a room and I've got a girl in there with me I'll pay the cash."

"This isn't any prostitution venture, mister."

"No? What is it then?"

"A nudist camp."

"Crap. I've been to those and nobody promises you anything in advance the way this Skip Bart did. You go and you shuck your clothes but when you're my age you don't get a tumble from the sloppiest bitch on the reservation. Try it alone and see what you get. You pick out some girl, you're nice to her, but when it comes to leading her to a mattress she's got a steady or a husband who does that for her."

Dutch spit into the grass.

"Lots of dames can be bought," he said.

"Naturally, but who wants them? Most of them have an assembly line production, so much time for each customer, and who hankers for that? Besides, I like the sun. A man needs it, just being out in the sun and air, and when he's got a girl with him who can ask for more? You sprawl on the grass during the day, the girl kind of close to you, making you feel important, and at night you know she's going to be yours."

"That's up to you," Dutch told the man. "I don't sell flesh and I don't trade in it."

"The pictures he showed me of the girls were great. Young, every one of them. Young and he said that a man could haul his freight. You haven't got much here but it could be in the city dump and it wouldn't stop me. I'd break with my wife tomorrow if she didn't control the money. That's the trouble with this country today. A man works but the woman has all of the power and she stomps him into the ground. She'll sleep with you when you're both young, more to start a family than anything else, but once she hits forty she moves into her own bedroom. You have to turn somewhere else but you have to be careful when you do."

"That's your difficulty," Dutch said. "Not mine."

"I like it here. I think I'll be seeing you."

"Whatever you decide is okay."

The man started for his car.

"I have decided. You've got the privacy and you'll have the girls. To be honest about it I need both."

Dutch watched the Caddy back out to the road and he got up from the steps. He didn't know much about a nudist camp, only what he had been told, but he didn't think that coming to one should be sold on the basis of available sex. Probably every camp had some form of sexual relationships. He didn't see how it could be avoided. A couple met in the nude, they liked each other, they saw what they were, and whatever they did was as natural as rain coming down from the sky.

He entered the kitchen and got a can of beer from the refrigerator. Frankly, he didn't like the way Skip Bart was handling things but maybe it would prove to be all right. There were swimming places in Europe where you had to be nude to go in but of course there was a much broader viewpoint about the human body in those countries than there was here at home.

"It's a terrible storm," that one girl in Iceland had told him when she had awakened him from a deep sleep. "I couldn't get home."

He had touched her, finding her naked in the bed with him.

"You're nude."

"What of it? I can't sleep in my clothes very well and you seem regular."

"Aren't you pressing your luck?"

"Not when you know somebody you like or feel that you should like. Just because we're here together doesn't mean that it's any more than that, does it?"

Of course it hadn't meant any more than that but it had been a night of mental strain and physical anguish. She had crept up against him, seeking to get warm, and she hadn't thought twice about her actions. It wasn't due to the fact that sex wasn't important to those people. It was just as important to them as to anybody else but it was looked upon as a desirable outlet for honest emotions and perhaps there was more honesty in their love. Here a man gave a girl a child and sometimes he either denied what he had done or he ran. Up there he did neither. He might or might not marry the girl but he supported the child.

Dutch was tired and he sat at the kitchen table, drinking the beer and looking at his checking account. That Cherry had busted a hole into it and if he let her continue he'd be scratching dirt in some farmer's garden for his room and board. It was the one thing about her, her demands for money, that dismayed him. Still, it wasn't too serious when he considered the balance he had in the bank. With luck, they'd earn it back during the summer—the spring, too, if the weather held up—and the old Ford should be able to make it south.

He killed the rest of the day, smoking and drinking beer. It was a waste of time. He didn't do anything that amounted to much when she was near him and he did just about the same when she was away.

It was about five when the car stopped outside. He didn't get up to see who it was. He knew. That fan belt on Penny's car was wearing out and it made a noise. If she didn't get it fixed the thing would break one of these days and she'd be walking along the road on her feet.

He grunted.

He should worry.

To hell with her car.

She came in without knocking and she reeked the sex that he had known through a tight skirt and a white blouse that revealed her naked breasts beneath the thin material. He kind of liked a girl who wasn't ashamed of herself and who was proud of what she had. Of course she needed a bra in town but out in the hills it was rather common for a girl to dress in such a manner.

"The girl isn't coming back tonight," Penny said. "She called and told me."

"Okay. Thanks."

"She bought cots."

"What did she spend?"

"I don't know. Would I ask that?"

"No, I suppose not." He left the table and opened a couple of cans of beer. "I'd have bet money that you would have told her where to go?"

"Get mad? Why should I?"

"Because of that day."

She accepted the beer but she remained standing.

"Can I help what you do?" she inquired. "I may not approve of the situation but can I help it?"

"Not very well."

He offered her a cigarette. She shook her head. It wasn't her brand. She had to have that menthol junk. Up in Iceland they'd been rationed on their cigarettes. He'd gotten into the habit of the king size because they lasted longer.

"You're a fool," she said. "I can't keep from telling you that."

"If I am I'll pay for it."

"No doubt."

"Am I crying? I paid for other things that I never got."

Her eyes clouded over with pain.

"Do you have to continue bringing that back to life, Dutch?"

"I guess I shouldn't," he admitted.

"That's better. You can't hurt me a great deal more than I've already been hurt. It's just that it doesn't belong between us."

"Whatever you say."

He resumed his seat at the table but she continued to stand, her feet slightly apart, the skirt snug and form fitting over her thighs.

"Some man with a Caddy stopped at the shack, asking about how he got up here."

"I saw him."

"Is he a nudist?"

"He talked as though he was."

"I felt him raping me with his eyes."

"Some men do that. When a girl has got a build she has to accept the consequences."

She finished her beer but she didn't ask for another one. She walked over to the refrigerator and got it herself.

"I'm done with my job," she said. "The lawyer phoned the shack and he didn't believe me. I had hoped a lawyer would look at it differently. Aren't you innocent until you're proven guilty?"

"Sometimes. You placed the guilt on me the other day and you didn't know what it was all about. You saw a situation and you came to your own conclusion as to what it was."

"Are you guilty now?"

"Of what?"

"Of being with her?"

"That's personal." He yawned. "So what about a new job?"

"Try and get one. I tried a few places but I need a reference. The only person I ever worked for was the lawyer and I can't give his name."

"You don't need to be honest to run a machine in some factory. Just say that you've lived home, watching the rest of the kids, and that you never worked before. They don't care who you are or where you come from in a factory. All they want is your blood."

She was standing close to him and he heard her let out a long breath.

"You don't know the factories in town, do you?"

"How could I? I was gone for two years and their jobs didn't amount to the price of gas to get to them when I left."

"Well, it's worse now. Most of them are on short time and if I drove back and forth I couldn't exist on what I'd earn."

Dutch glanced up at her. He felt that he didn't have any use for her but Cherry was in the city and he could get very busy with her if she gave him the chance.

"I told you how to turn a dollar," he said.

Her eyes met his and held.

"You'd like that wouldn't you?" she challenged him.

"What you do is your own affair."

"You didn't act that way before."

"You're wrong. You just thought I didn't."

She acted as though she was going to cry.

"Then you only came to me to—"

"Be sensible, Penny." He was annoyed. "What you gave I took and if I hadn't taken it you'd have given it to somebody else. Don't kid me. Once a girl has been with a man she knows that the best place in life is on the flat of her back."

She turned away from him in disgust.

"You're filthy."

"I don't give a damn what I am. I think what I want and I say what I think. Years ago I didn't used to be that way. I was taught to respect a girl but I learned that it paid off with a kick in the guts. I—"

"Shut up!" she screamed, wheeling to face him. Her lips curled viciously. "I'm sick and tired of hearing what's wrong with me and what's so good about you. Who are you anyway? You're just a big slob who didn't have the courage to understand when I made a mistake. If you had loved me you would have understood or at least there would have been some sympathy. What did I get? Can you answer that?"

"You got what you deserved."

"Did I? Not from you I didn't. I planned to marry Cliff, to divorce him as soon as the baby had a name and come back to you on my hands and beg you to forgive me. I'd have given up the child if you had insisted. I wanted it fine and wonderful between us. But where were you? Off in some foreign country and I was stuck with a hopeless marriage. I decided to try and make it work and I did try. I'm no angel but I doubt if any girl ever tried harder. I failed but when I failed I learned more about life than you know. Life to you is simply a matter of sleeping with a girl, of satisfying yourself. So you put yourself above me, up in the clouds. But are you above me? Are you?"

"Get out," he said hotly. "Or are you going to take up a collection for the sermon?" He reached into his pocket. "Here's a dime. I'll take two cents in change."

"Damn you!" She was nearly hysterical. "Oh, damn you and every man who ever walked!"

He threw the dime at her. It landed on the floor. Sobbing, she picked it up and flung it from her.

"Get out," he said again.

She choked down her sobs and laughed at him. "Don't I get your rotten job?"

"Not when you're in this mood."

She reached for the front of her blouse with one hand.

"What do you want?" she demanded.

"Whatever you've got."

"As long as it's free?"

"Sure. Why pay for used merchandise?"

"Don't pretend that she hasn't been used."

"Drop dead!" he shouted, rising to his feet. "Hit the door or I'll bust you in the mouth."

Her laugh haunted the years that hung between them.

"You pig, there's only one bust you want. Maybe she's bigger than I am but she isn't here. She's—"

Penny ripped at the blouse and tore it from her body. Naked above the waist, her breasts heaving, swollen, she taunted him with her smile.

"Hey, now—"

"It's your turn to shut up, Dutch." She lifted her hands to her breasts, cupping them. "I love you, you stinking creep, but the rest is up to you. What's mine is yours, no matter where it ends, but I'm not going to plead. I'll tend your miserable stand. I'll go nude and let them see me. My pride is gone. Next to my family, you're all I've got and now I haven't got you."

Cherry...

In the city...

Beautiful Cherry...

Lovely Penny…

It wasn't love as he fought with her clothes. It was the male beast, tortured beyond endurance—the male beast that cared for only one thing, knew only one thing, understood only one thing.

Need…

Overpowering and terrible…

A half hour later he left her broken and spent in the living room, half off of the sofa and half on it.

He sat in the kitchen and had a beer, listening to her cry alone and, for the moment, unwanted. There was no sense to it but he cried himself. He didn't know why.

He didn't finish all of the beer.

Dutch felt terrible.

6

SOMEHOW, DURING THE next few weeks, they managed to get the work done. Most of Dutch's work was outside and Penny helped Cherry in the house. The girls weren't friends and that worried him. He didn't see why they shouldn't be friends but they weren't.

It was necessary for him to hire others to do various jobs and because of strangers on the grounds they wore their clothes so as not to cause gossip. The plumbers were curious about the bathroom facilities in the barn but he merely told them he was thinking of starting a resort for kids. One of the locals who was too stupid to know the difference between daylight and darkness hung up curtains in the barn to separate some of the cots and provide a degree of privacy for those who wished to enjoy the finer, frequently forbidden, pleasures of life.

The bad part was that everything cost money. Lawn chairs had to be purchased and even the few games they ordered amounted to a considerable sum. The cost of the boats was high and the equipment in the snack bar wasn't delivered for nothing. He began to realize that the venture had to pay off or he might as well set fire to the whole business and watch it burn.

"It's shaping up," Cherry said one night. "It really is."

"I wish things were in as good a shape as you're in."

She laughed.

"Fresh."

"No. I mean it. The weather is great but what if it changes? Get a rainy spell and I won't lose my shirt — it'll already be lost. And we don't hear from Skip. I could stand that, believe me, but now we have to depend on the guy."

"Don't worry. He'll come through."

"Something had better come through or I'll be going back to that pile of rocks in the North Atlantic again — if there's a job. I could do without that and that's no lie."

They were in the living room and she came over to sit down on his lap. One arm crept around his neck and her lips hovered near his mouth.

"Anyway we got the phone put in, Dutch."

"So people can call us to collect money. Yeah. We should hide under the rocks."

"Stop being silly. I wrote Skip and we'll be getting calls. We — did you get those reservation cards printed?"

"No. Tomorrow."

"Phone the man now."

He bruised her lips with a kiss.

"Forget him. Right this second I'm about to become very busy."

"Pig."

"But you like pigs."

Her lips were warm, eager.

"I love pigs. Your kind."

It was the same every night, always the same, their anxious bodies merging, the moans and sighs in the bedroom, the final conclusion that left him exhausted.

Yes. it was good — and it wasn't. He didn't know why it wasn't good, unless he was changing and he felt there should be more to their lives than mere pleasure that erupted from a physical force. He had an almost terrible urge to have the ground solid beneath his feet, to understand where he was going and how he could get there. Days, when he was working alone, it bothered him, yet at night he could forget these problems with her.

The weather...

Well, they had to count on that. A cold summer of frequent rains could destroy them. Nobody ran around naked when they half froze to death. He had read a little bit about nudist camps and those that operated during the winter weren't, during that period, nudist camps at all. They had club houses where they drank and talked but they didn't take off their clothes. Some camps were split up into two parts, one a reservation where clothing was frowned upon and the other, the social section, where being dressed was a must. He appreciated this thought because the basic search of the nudist was to enjoy the sun, to gain health from it, and not to go nude for the mere sake of being that way. A number of experts estimated there were at least a million nudists in the country, although about half of these practiced it in private and didn't belong to any organization. The majority of camps had very strict rules, leaning more to the role of catering to families rather than the individual.

"They do it their way," Cherry said. "We'll do it our way. Our charge is a hundred and fifty dollars for a single male guest and seventy-five for a female. What if the men come up here to look? They're the same men who'd go to a burlesque show if one was playing, the ones who buy the nudes I used to pose for. Leave them on the streets, frustrated, and you've got a rape in the making. Make it easy for them to come up here and they get it out of their system."

The printer acted cool when he went into town to pick up the reservation cards.

"High View Nudist Camp," he said. "Somebody blew the spokes out of one of their wheels."

"What other use does the place have?"

"That isn't the point. We just haven't had that sort of a thing around here before. Maybe we've got no progress in the county but you can't say this is a way of getting ahead."

"I paid you, didn't I?"

"Of course."

"So forget about it. You work for a living and so do I. If you offered me your printing shop I wouldn't take it as a gift but that doesn't mean there shouldn't be printers."

Cherry called him just as he was getting ready to leave. Skip was arriving on the noon bus and would he wait and pick up the guy? He said he would and carried the printed forms out to the car.

There was a bar opposite the bus terminal and he stopped in for a few drinks. He didn't actually need anything to drink at that time of the morning but it was one of the habits which he had acquired since his return to the farm.

"Stinking hot," the girl behind the bar said and drew his beer.

She was a fat, sloppy girl, big in the bust and her arms were loaded with excess weight. Maybe she was twenty or twenty-five. He couldn't guess because she could have been almost any age from nineteen to thirty.

He drank his beer and paid little attention to her. Feeling as he did nearly every morning or when he was alone he was sorry that he'd ever gotten into this nudist thing. He simply couldn't follow the reasoning of a nudist in spite of all of the claims that were made in favor of the movement. He thought that it was all right for a man to be nude with the girl he loved, that it was both accepted and expected, but for a group of strangers to desire getting together that way was a little amazing for his mind that still wasn't conditioned to the fullest extent. He was aware that the sun gave off beneficial rays, that these were absorbed through the skin, that without the sun there would be a great deal of illness and perhaps not even life. Then why not the beach or a lawn where people sprawled out in skimpy costumes? Silly, the nudists said. The sun couldn't probe through material and reach the most important organs of a human being. That was a mystery to him, this reasoning, and he concluded it would always be. To Dutch, being nude meant sex and nothing more. How could people be in close contact with each other and escape it? Yet he had noticed one thing. A naked girl didn't create the same impression or generate the impulses of the male quite as much as the girl who wore very little. Once they were stripped there was nothing left for the imagination to dwell upon, nothing hidden that couldn't be seen.

Shortly before twelve he walked over to wait for the bus. A man with a suitcase tied up with a rope was also waiting. He was chewing tobacco and some of it ran down his chin. He wiped it away with the back of one hand and more appeared.

A drifter...

Maybe, Dutch thought, he'd look like that by September. Next to being broke, five bucks a fortune, beating along the roads for a job.

Maybe...

Ten thousand dollars. A lot of money? Not much when you spent it, slept with someone you loved, bought the girl what she wanted, wasn't too particular what you did. Chances. The world was filled with them just as it was filled with people. Too many people, they said. Not enough to eat, they said. A mess.

The bus rattled in. It was an old bus, dug up from a junk yard, one of those things the company used when it ran short because of charter runs.

Skip Bart got off, carrying a briefcase and his camera. He smiled when he saw Dutch but even the smile didn't make his face appear friendly. There was something about the fellow that was cold, a deadly vacancy in his eyes that concealed whatever he was actually thinking.

"They can shove that bus," he said as he got into the Ford. "If they can't I'll help them."

"Well, you can't have everything?"

"Who wants it?"

Dutch hit the curb as he pulled away from it.

"How's things in the city?" he wanted to know.

"Moving."

"For us?"

"Hell, fellow, you know it."

"Do you mind telling me?"

"Not at all. Guys. A flock of them."

"And girls?"

"They're no problem. For twenty bucks they'd get into a casket with a corpse and try to bring the poor jerk back to life."

Dutch scowled.

"I'm concerned about having that type of girl up here."

"Are you going to sleep with them?"

"Of course not."

"So? Everybody registers and it's legal. You get your fee and I take my cut from what they sell. The thing is to have more men than girls. If you even it out a girl can't keep herself busy and when a girl isn't busy I don't make any money. What charity do you think I'm running?"

"You talk like a pimp," Dutch decided.

"Take that back, guy. I'm no pimp. I find men and I know girls. The men want the girls and I get them together. Is that a crime? All I earn is a few bucks."

"All right. You're no pimp but I can't see why a man has to go to all of this trouble and expense to enjoy himself."

"That's because you don't know what I know. These men are married and they're important. Rock them with a scandal and they'd be flat on their rumps. So they can't hardly trust anybody. They have to be sure. If they throw a fast one at a secretary it can cost them. Their best bet is to tell their wives that they're going away on a business trip. Instead of doing that they spend a few days or a week up here and they have their choice."

Dutch grunted. He wasn't pleased by the whole arrangement but he was into it too deep to quit. If he'd only talked it over with Cherry before they'd gone this far, convinced her that it wasn't sense — but he hadn't. And, legally, he supposed he wasn't doing anything so very wrong. He merely provided the opportunity and the men and girls would make the most of it. He was no worse than a hotel owner who rented a room to an unmarried couple.

"Some man was up here in a Caddy," Dutch said as they reached the mountain road.

"Yeah. His wife is rich."

"So I gathered."

"She's a dried up fig. Clubs, society, the works. And as sexless as a cold night in January."

"Where do you find these men?"

"Christ, you ask a lot of questions."

"I'm merely curious."

"That's bad sometimes."

"It isn't the only thing that's bad."

"They — well, some of them come to me for nude studies. They can buy them by the pound almost anywhere but there are laws and a girl can just show so much. That type of photo I sell to magazines but the others, the real thing, I save for private collections. Maybe a guy sees the picture of one particular girl and he goes nuts about her. On the average he wouldn't stand a chance of ever meeting her. The actual pros take their sex outside with a steady and posing is simply a job for them. But there are other girls you can get who don't care what they do or who they do it with. They're selling a product, their bodies, and there's always a market."

"Why bother with a nudist camp? I came close to asking that before but I still don't get the point."

"Atmosphere."

"That answers most of it."

"Rolling fields. A lake. A day in the sun with some broad that's naked, plus a choice of a sleeping companion. What choice does a man have when he picks up a prostitute? The girl may look great but the guy might have to throw her falsies away before he can find her. Then there are girdles and once that's off she may sag like the stock market in a depression. At a nudist camp he doesn't have to guess. He knows. He weighs the meat with his eyes and buys what he wants. Add to this the men who are past that stage of life. I'd say the man with the Caddy could be one. All he wants to do is look, that type of man. He's half dead and he knows it but he thinks he's going to get a second lease on life. He takes pills or shots and they don't help. He thinks this will. He's stupid — but he's got money. All we want is his money."

"I kind of wish I wasn't into this," Dutch said as they neared the farm.

"Don't wish. You are in it."

"How well I know."

"At the end of the season you'll thank me."

"Or be in jail."

He swung into the driveway and parked the Ford behind Penny's car. The plumber's truck was down near the barn. They were taking their time all right, running up his bill.

Penny stood at the bottom of the back steps.

She wore a faded dress but the tightness of the dress complimented her figure.

"Some blonde," Skip said.

"She's okay."

"A friend of yours?"

"I guess you could say that."

"Any chance of her —"

"No."

They got out of the car and Dutch smiled at Penny as they passed her and went up the steps. Her lips remained in a firm, tense line. She had avoided him since that wild night in the living room and he had stayed away from her as much as possible. What he had done to her, no different than what he had done before except more savage, weighed heavily inside of him. Maybe it wasn't so much because of his actions but because he had violated Cherry's love.

"Where's Cherry?" Skip asked once they were in the kitchen. "I came up here to level things out with her."

"She must be around the house."

"Mind if I look?"

"Help yourself."

Skip placed his briefcase on the kitchen table and disappeared. Thoughtfully, Dutch regarded the briefcase. It was partly open due to a broken zipper and the corner of a small binder stuck outside.

Dutch removed the binder and glanced through it. There were some photos of the farm but mostly the pictures were of naked girls. He was pleased to note there were none of Cherry but a picture of one girl drew his careful attention.

The girl he had met that night in the bar, his first night back in the states.

The girl he hadn't touched.

He returned the binder to the briefcase, his mind churning. It didn't add up correctly, drinking with Skip, not sure at all of what he said, meeting the girl, now seeing her picture and well, perhaps it did add. If Skip was acquainted with the girl, which was certainly true, he could have been drinking with her and they could have separated. There was no harm in that, was there?

A horn blew and Dutch went outside. It was the man delivering the grill for the snack bar, along with a tank of gas, and he rode down to the building in the truck with the man.

"You should have ordered two tanks of gas," the man said.

"Why?"

"Well, if one runs out you've got a reserve. This way you're licked."

"Thanks. Bring one out."

"Next week."

"That's time enough."

He helped the man hook up the stove, read the instructions so he'd know how to use it and then, after the man left, got into the paint again. There wasn't much more that had to be done to the stand and he wanted to complete the job. The next thing would be supplies and that would cut deeper into his money. Actually, there was a need for a refrigerator but unless he could get a used one in fair condition they'd have to manage with-out it.

He thought of Skip up there at the house with Cherry but it didn't cause him any worry. They could handle the details of getting customers to come to the camp and Cherry was the kind of a girl who required a man. He grinned and slapped the paint on the boards. All man and then some. Never fully satisfied, always willing and demanding, lifting in passion, giving in fury. Assuming that she'd consent to have him Slim could never take care of that black haired beauty.

When he was through painting he looked over his work. The snack bar was no prize in construction but it could be worse. You couldn't remodel anything with cheap lumber and have a masterpiece.

"Dutch!"

He turned. He hadn't been aware of Penny's approach but when he saw her face he grinned. Her face was hot and wild, her eyes clouded with concern. What if she craved what she had offered that night, what he had taken in lust, what he had hated himself for later? Yes, what of it? He was no angel and he didn't pretend to be one.

"What gives?" he asked.

"She took that monster back to town."

"I didn't hear the car but it's fine with me."

She leaned against the counter and got some fresh paint on her arms.

"I hate him," she said bluntly.

"He's no friend of mine."

"Wondering if I'd pose in the nude for him. What do I look like?"

"I thought I warned him about that."

She rubbed at the paint on her arms.

"Well, I won't warn him the next time. He doesn't know the kind of girls that grow in the hills. I'll pick up a rock and smash him in the head just to find out if he's got any brains." She paused. "And that Cherry, too. Open up her skull and you'll come up with nothing but sex."

"Now, Penny—"

"She's no good. I mean it, Dutch. She's no good and she's destroying you. You're spending your money and you'll lose any reputation you might have around here."

"You lost yours."

"Yes, and I paid for it. Somebody said that you pay in sweat, blood and tears. I know how hard it is to pay that way, what you go through and I don't want that for you. Maybe you're not mine but I'm yours. When you're hurt I'm hurt."

"I can take care of myself."

"When you're up against a beautiful girl?"

"Skip it."

Her lips curled.

"You're up against her all right. Every night."

"You weren't too difficult yourself." His tone was brutal.

"Because it was love. Because — Dutch, listen to me."

"I'm listening."

"I should have — well, you know."

"Sorry, I don't know."

"Nor do I."

"You don't make sense. What is this? A riddle?"

This time when she leaned upon the counter she didn't pay any attention to the fresh paint.

"It was the same with Cliff," she said.

"What?"

"Soon. Just once and I was that way."

It was a hot day but he suddenly felt cold all over.

"Stop dreaming," he said.

She nodded.

"I guess I shouldn't worry you."

"No."

"But if I am it's yours and I want you to know."

She left the stand and walked up toward the house. He lit a cigarette and choked on the smoke. What she had hinted at didn't seem possible but he knew that such things were possible. Year in and year out girls found themselves in that condition, their stomachs swollen, their hopes shattered, either deserted by the men responsible or bound to them in a common misery.

He gagged on the cigarette and followed her up to the house. He found her in one of the bedrooms, washing windows. She resisted as he swung her sharply and brought her in tight.

"Then there are no more worries," he said, knowing that their worries had only started.

"Please, Dutch. No. Not for the sake of being used. Not because she's out of the house and there's nobody here."

"If you love me the way you say you do it's real."

She stared up into his face.

"I love you for what you could be."

"But not for what I am?"

"Every girl draws a line. She —"

He ignored her and pushed her toward the bed. She fought for a moment, then gave up. She was like nothing at all in his arms.

But he didn't touch her.

He ran from her and plunged into the bathroom. Sweat covered him all over.

He was very sick.

Sick because he hated his own guts.

7

THEY GOT A few guests the following weekend, some girls and men, and everybody went naked. It wasn't the best weather for the people to run around in nothing except their skin but the sun was hot during the day and the people didn't seem to mind. A few even went in swimming but they didn't stay long.

Dutch's first experience in the open without his clothes on wasn't as difficult as he had assumed it would be. When everybody was nude it just came naturally as being the thing to do.

"It isn't so rough, is it?" Dutch said to Penny when he stopped at the stand for coffee.

"Rough? It's the most awful situation I've ever seen."

She was behind the counter, her breasts bared to the open, the contours of them perfect, inviting.

"Want to quit?"

"No, Dutch."

"I don't want you to think —"

"That I have to do it? But I do. It isn't the money alone. Honest. You have to find yourself one of these days and I'm going to be right there with you when it happens."

"I've found myself."

"With her? How could you?"

He drank his coffee.

"Don't be the jealous female, Penny."

"I'm not jealous — well, yes, I am — but I was foolish. Twice in a row and not a brain in my head."

He departed from the stand. Lately, he'd spent hours in a blue funk, concerned about her, about himself. What if she — he shook his head as he crossed the field. Yes, what if she was? What if the chickens came home to roost and he was living in the chicken coop? It would be a disaster, pure and simple. A physical and emotional disaster for which he wasn't prepared. Marriage? Of course marriage — but to Cherry and nobody else. Marriage to Cherry and having her for himself for as long as they were each permitted to breathe.

The group that was gathered near the beach was an odd assortment of human beings. A couple of the men had good builds but for the most part they had beer fat or some other kind of fat around their stomachs. The girls were altogether different. They were young, very beautiful, their curves and laughter promising the ultimate in satisfaction. Crazy girls, he thought, on the loose, lacking moral restraint, their favors available to the highest bidder.

"Say, you're a big guy," one girl said to him. "Were you ever a fighter in the ring?"

She was a brunette, rather short in height but long on natural appeal. Her breasts were separated by a beautiful valley, the lifting crests on either side of her cleavage wealthy with the flesh that put money in the bank for her.

"No, I never fought in any ring."

"Bet you could smash somebody into a pulp, huh?"

"Maybe. You can't always be a winner."

She jerked her head.

"See that man over there? The one with the bald head?"

"Yeah."

"What girl would want him?"

The man looked like some creature that had crawled up out of the lake, neither human nor animal.

"I don't know," Dutch confessed.

"He says I'm his."

"That your deal."

"If it was I wouldn't be here. A hotel room is okay if the guy is okay but not this. This is where you fall off the end of the bridge."

"Nobody twisted your arm."

"Didn't they? You don't know the half of it. Or a third. Or nothing at all."

"I'm willing to learn."

"Fine only I'm no teacher. I'm just bitching." She rubbed one of her thighs with her hand. "Where's Skip?"

"Coming up on the afternoon bus. Or the train. He sounded drunk when he phoned."

"Drunk? Or on the weed?"

"Does he use that?"

"Sometimes. Not often but he does when he's feeling nervous."

Dutch shifted his weight from one foot to the other. The only thing he had on was a pair of sneaks. The girl was barefooted and her nails were painted, not red but sort of a silver color.

"I guess you like Skip," he said.

"Let me laugh, will you? That guy is a crumb."

"Then why have anything to do with him?"

"I might have a reason."

"Maybe you do."

"But he's no worse than the Princess."

"I don't know of any Princess."

"You'll find out."

"It would save time if you'd tell me."

The girl laughed.

"Yes, but I won't."

He wandered around after that, thinking. Nothing was right and everything was wrong. He knew what wasn't right, throwing these girls to the men, but when it came to the total wrongness he was stuck. Yet it was there, an evil thing that would get more evil with each passing day. On the other hand —

Fine. All right. On the other hand — what of it? There wasn't any other hand. There was just this. Even with a small crowd the fees amounted to quite a bit. The girls didn't pay to enter. The men paid for that. They would have paid for the same thing in the city, perhaps less but they would have paid. Flesh sold by the ounce or the ton, it all amounted to the same thing. A man slept with a girl and he had the pleasure of her favors. He paid for it, either here on the farm or somewhere else. Scenery didn't change morals. It didn't change—

But it did. It changed a lot of things, not the location of the act but the thinking of the individual who became a part of it. Sex for money had never particularly appealed to Dutch. It was like buying a car that had been used or wrecked, the joys which other men had known and for which money had been spent. Sex, as an outlet of need, he regarded in a different light. People got hungry and they ate. People also desired love, as much to be loved as to love, and they sought it out. They met their own kind and what they did was their affair.

How, he asked himself, had he arrived at a moment in his life when he walked naked through soft grass, when other naked people were near him, when a worthy cause, depending upon the viewpoint, was being ridiculed and disgraced? Perhaps it was a lengthy question but it had a simple answer. A bar. Too much to drink. A prostitute who hadn't found it necessary to earn her money. Another bar the next day. A beautiful girl and a casual conversation, his gears meshing with hers because of what he felt he must gain from her. Money. This farm. Probably too interested in pleasing the girl to weigh all of the facts in their proper sequence: When you had ten thousand dollars you didn't worry about going down to nine.

You didn't even worry when your bank account hit seven thousand. But at two thousand you worried and you were caught.

He stopped for another coffee.

"The rooms are filled up at the house," he said to Penny.

Coldly, she received this information.

"Should I cheer?" she inquired with the same coldness that was in her eyes.

"Do what you want. I only said. The nights would be pretty cold in the barn."

"They won't be cold."

"Probably not."

"What would you tell the police if they came?"

He scratched his head.

"Yeah," he admitted. "Yeah, what would I tell them?"

"Just what you'll probably tell me when I'm positive that you're going to be a father."

"You're guessing ahead of me, aren't you?"

"Of course. You'll tell me nothing." She poured a coffee for herself. "Well, I don't want anything if you're not willing to give it to me."

"I gave you enough already."

Her eyes flashed anger.

"Don't be crude, Dutch."

He glanced across the field toward the lake.

"You don't have to have any kid," he said.

He felt the hot coffee she had drawn strike him in the head. He pawed at the heat with his hands and cursed her.

"Never say that to me again, Dutch."

"Hey, Penny — "

"Leave me alone." She was close to tears. "Can't you see that? Leave me alone and go to her. I'll work for my wages but that's all I ask. I — no, that isn't all. I want you to be a man Animals belong in cages. Animals should — "

He walked away from her. The coffee still burned and he cursed some more. Something or somebody had made her a different person. Maybe he had done it but perhaps Cliff had altered her. Or the death of her child. Females were funny that way. They carried a baby they didn't want for nine months but once it was born they'd die for it. At least some would. A few weren't human. Beasts. As much or more than a man.

When he reached the house he entered the kitchen. Cherry was at one of the windows, stripped down naked to her bare feet.

"Isn't it great?" she wanted to know.

"Great? Baby, you tell me."

"I said not to call me that."

"Yeah. I forgot."

"You're excused. What I meant was those people down there. Getting the sun, being just ordinary people. Freedom. Go into the city and see what you find. Fifty dollar a week clerks wearing clothes that aren't paid for, trying to make an impression on anybody who wants to notice them. That's existing but it isn't life."

Dutch got a beer from the refrigerator.

"I don't like it," he said, his mind stumbling.

"You don't like the money?"

"Who hates money?"

"You tell me."

"One person. The guy who doesn't have it."

She looked out of the window again.

"This weekend is just a tiny sample, Dutch. It's the same as the two of us together. The more we get of what's the best the more we want." She moved so that he had a perfect profile of her. "Or haven't I got what sends you?"

"Baby, you know better than that."

"There it goes again. Baby."

His insides dropped until he thought they had hit his knees. Baby. Penny. Perhaps a child that was both unwanted and unloved. Baby. The extreme folly for not being smart, for being too human and careless. He put the can of beer down, unfinished. What could he do if that should be true? Certainly his suggestion to her had been pretty low, cutting Penny when she didn't deserve it. Any decent girl desired the life that was inside of her to come screaming into the world. Only the tramps took any other attitude. And Penny wasn't a tramp, no matter what she had done.

"What if you were going to have one?" he asked Cherry.

"Please. Don't shock me."

"It could happen."

She picked up the can of beer he had discarded.

"Doesn't any girl know that, Dutch?"

"Suppose she does. She'd have to be ignorant not to realize there's a price for everything." He walked to the table and sat down. "I've got to talk to you, Cherry. We're sinking into a hole and I want to know how we can get out of it."

"I don't follow you."

"Then sit down."

She did. There across the table from him she looked more beautiful than ever.

"You've been worried lately, haven't you?" she asked. "I can see it. Sometimes you mumble in your sleep."

"Yes, I'm worried. That's a fact."

"There's nothing to worry about."

"Isn't there?"

"No."

There was a pack of cigarettes on top of the table and he took one.

"It's what's going on up here that bothers me."

She smiled.

"Dutch, stop making an issue out of empty air. These people come to the farm and we get our fee. So what if they do something wrong? Do we have to hold their hands?"

He shook his head.

"I understand that but it just goes against my grain. As far as a nudist camp goes I'm not prejudiced toward it or in favor of the thing. They exist and I'd be the last one in the world to fight the issue. I feel there is some merit to their way of thinking but I do know that what they think is clean. This isn't."

"Which brings us back to the money, doesn't it?"

"Money I had."

"Not now."

"A little. We couldn't do much with it but I could sell the farm and we'd have that. The land isn't worth much but the lake is a big factor. What if we only got twenty thousand? It's enough for us to move on. Lots of people do it on seventy-five bucks."

She leaned forward, her breasts pushing out.

"That isn't the only reason," she said.

"No."

"Can't you level with me?"

"Sure. It's Skip Bart. I don't trust the guy and I didn't from the start. He's too interested in us and I don't figure why. How can it pay him a fair profit for his time."

"The men pay him."

"Which is a form of prostitution."

She leaned back, looking good.

"People are people, Dutch."

"I'd be a fool to deny it."

"You seem to think that if you had twenty thousand dollars you'd be rich."

"Far from it."

"Well, you wouldn't. I know what we'd do if you went ahead and sold out. There'd be a trip and a car and we wouldn't work. We'd take care of each other in every hotel along the road. In the end we'd be somewhere and we'd be broke. You'd get a job but then we'd come to hate each other because we'd be used to spending money and we wouldn't have it. I — Dutch, I don't want that for us. I don't want the poverty that I saw in the coal fields."

"The work I do pays a big salary," he insisted.

"Maybe but we'd be moving all the time. We'd never be able to plant our roots and become a part of a community. Would you want our kids to go to ten different schools? I know I don't. I'm satisfied here and we can make a killing."

"But —"

"Dutch, where's your nerve? If somebody took a swing at you you'd fight back. You wouldn't care what you used as long as you won, would you? All right. We're fighting. We're fighting the world together for money and this is the quickest way of getting it. Do you want twenty thousand or a hundred or more?"

"I want you," he replied.

"You've got me. You've had me and I'm yours whenever you need me."

He felt depressed. She would give of herself, surrendering her body to him, but she would have to be very understanding if anything was wrong with Penny. A girl might love but few could forgive that. He hadn't forgiven Penny, had he? Why was the shoe on the other foot different.

"We'll try it your way," he said finally.

"Do you want to meet Skip?"

"I guess somebody should."

"He phoned. It's the train this time. He missed the bus."

"He isn't too well liked," Dutch told her, remembering the girl down by the lake.

"Everybody has enemies. They grow as fast as crab grass in a lawn. Most of the people who don't like somebody else couldn't tell you just why they don't. When they put their dislike into words it seldom holds up."

He arose from the table and she did the same.

"Do I have to get anything in town?"

"Not that I can think of."

He stepped close and grinned down at her.

"I know what I'd like to get. Right now."

She laughed and avoided his kiss.

"Later."

"Aw, what's a few minutes?"

She crossed the kitchen to the door.

"I'm going down to the lake."

"With that figure you'll get raped," he said.

She turned to smile at him.

"Would you mind?"

"I'd kill the slob. There wouldn't be any trial. Just a funeral. They could try me."

As soon as she was gone he went upstairs to dress. While he tied his shoes he sat on the edge of the bed. Their bed. Their bed where the darkness of the night held them in a tight embrace.

It was still early to drive to the railroad station and, fully clothed he stretched out on the bed. This was the room which he had occupied during much of his youth and for some strange reason a few of the memories of that period returned to him. His father had been a little foolish in trying to make a living from the barren soil but it was the only fault he'd had. Both of his parents had been sincere and honest. Even when money had been short they had supported their church and went to church each Sunday. What would they do if it was possible for them to know what the farm had become? He didn't have to guess about that. They'd hate him and die all over again.

He began to sweat.

Penny.

Tragedy had walked through her life and perhaps he had brought more to her. Revenge? He didn't consider that just then. If she bore his child it was an obligation that he'd have to face.

To run or to ignore it was to deny that he was a man. Onions? Why was he thinking of them? Onions were so much a pound, depending on the season. Well, the pleasures of the flesh cost money, too. No matter what a man took out of life he had to pay for it. Nobody could avoid that. Yes, the price of onions and the price of desire. So totally unrelated and, yet, in cost so much the same.

A nudist…

What was a nudist?

He thought he knew. A nudist, although not always accepted by society, was a person of firm and decent convictions. They held the sun in the highest regard but they respected it, too. The strength of the sun probed their bodies, brought them pleasure. There was little of the excitement that existed here on the farm, the frantic search for sex that had no moral foundation. The men who came to the farm were driven by raw lust, the girls who displayed themselves on the prowl for money.

He slept but he was soon awakened by voices in the hall. A man and a girl, the man pleading, the girl laughing. Outside his door, in his own home, arriving at a satisfactory price. A tragedy far greater than the one Penny had experienced. The tragedy of sex.

Nobody was around when he left the house and he drove slowly toward town. He was miserable and the misery clawed at him. Why couldn't he show Cherry that the right way was the only way? Yet who was he to show anybody the right way? So much of what he had done was wrong and disgusting. No, he couldn't show her. He had lost the ability to do that through bitterness.

The train was late and he sat on an express wagon, waiting.

Twenty minutes behind time the train pulled in. "How are all of my naked friends?" Skip asked as he came up to Dutch.

"Naked."

"You get a kick out of it?"

"No, I'm afraid I don't."

They walked to the Ford and Skip put his camera on the back seat.

"Well, you wouldn't. Once you've seen Cherry you've seen them all."

"Perhaps."

"Don't hand me any line, Dutch. You've been having that so much you wouldn't know what to do with another girl."

Dutch started the car.

"This whole thing stinks," he said. "Like a dead fish."

"I'll hold my nose."

"I don't care what you do but it does stink. Maybe if we changed our policy and catered to families —"

"Crap. You want the whole loaf of bread or just one slice?"

"Probably I'd rather do with the slice."

"You're a sucker to think that."

"Fine. I'm a sucker."

Skip didn't speak again until they were out of town.

"That blonde who works for you," he said. "She's got a pair."

"Anything you have in mind, is impossible."

"Why? She's just a dame, isn't she?"

"Forget it."

"Yeah. I understand. She's private stock. Once again you're a sucker. None of them are private. They were put here to be used — or use a man."

Dutch gripped the steering wheel.

"Believe me," he said. He was getting mad. "Believe me, you've got a mind so low that if you wore a hat you'd lose it."

"You'll find out how low it is."

"I don't have to find out. I already know."

But he wondered if he did. There was something about this whole affair that escaped him. He didn't think this was out of the ordinary. Whatever a person did there was always a motive for it and sometimes the motive was difficult to determine immediately.

Quite frequently the true motive was never discovered.

He glanced at Skip Bart.

It was an unpleasant thought.

8

IT RAINED THE following weekend and they didn't have any guests. There was nothing to do except sit around and drink and curse the weather. Skip phoned from the city and he was in a sour mood. Dutch didn't know why he should be. He wasn't losing anything.

They tried to relax in the living room and Dutch fooled with the old television set.

"Somebody busted it," he said to Cherry.

She yawned and spread herself out on the sofa.

"Maybe a tube burned out."

"Yeah. Sure."

He prowled the living room, pausing at each window to stare out at the rain. It was a cold rain and it slanted against the side of the house. It was even cold in the room and for that reason they were wearing clothes.

"Don't be so nervous, Dutch."

"Why wouldn't I be nervous? We need the money. That coat — hell, did you need a coat at this time of the year? Did it have to cost so much, huh?"

"It always clears," she said, not answering his question.

He dismissed the coat from his mind. A thousand dollars and it was supposed to be a bargain. It was his own fault. She had wanted the thing but he could have put it off. Only he hadn't. She'd been too real there in the bed with him and he'd promised.

"I'm still confused about last weekend," he told her.

"What's so confusing?

"The men."

"Aren't most men confusing?"

"After they've had a good time?"

"I wouldn't know."

They were drinking screwdrivers and she had some of his.

"With the exception of one they were distant," he said. "I asked them if they were coming back again and they all were pretty firm that they weren't. I've read a couple of your books on nudists and that isn't the usual pattern. When a nudist likes a place he comes back whenever he can."

"That's the confirmed nudist, darling. These men aren't. They came up here for a purpose and they got what they wanted. I keep explaining to you that being nude has very little to do with sex but you can't seem to get it through your head."

"Skip was taking pictures of everybody."

"He's a bug on that."

"And he's nuts. I don't think he should take them. How does anybody know how he'll use the pictures?"

"Isn't that his affair?"

"No. And I'd rather that he didn't come up here any more."

"Swell. We'll eat grass for food. Cows live on it so perhaps we can."

"It would be better than having trouble."

"There'll be no trouble," she assured him.

"You've got too much faith in luck. There are two kinds of luck, Cherry. Good and bad."

"Nonsense. And let's not fool ourselves, Dutch. He's got the customers for us and without them we're done. We could sit here on our hands without the help of the rain."

"There's road construction a few miles out of town."

She sat up quickly.

"Go ahead and build your damned road."

"Now you're angry."

"Yes. Angry with you and practical about us. He's got over a hundred men lined up already and the girls are willing."

"Too willing. They're bums."

"But beautiful."

"Granted but I hate to see those guys hanging around you with their eyes out of the sockets."

"Window dressing," she explained.

"Well, it disgusts me."

"It doesn't when I'm with you in the bedroom."

"That's another matter."

"You'll never make a nudist."

He thought about this.

"I don't know," he said. "Perhaps I would if the circumstances were different. I see nothing but filth here and I revolt against it. This is a shocker that hauls off and hits you right between the eyes. We should have approached the whole thing from another direction. If a person wants to be a nudist that's no concern of mine and if I happen to have a suitable area I wouldn't object to taking money from them. This — well, this is a switch that violates everything human."

"Honey, those screwdrivers are tearing your brains apart."

"It isn't the screwdrivers. It's what I feel."

Her eyes were wide and serious.

"Don't you want me, Dutch?"

"Yes. Yes, I want you."

"In some cheap apartment where we can't even pay the rent?"

"No, not that."

"Then can't you do this for me? Can't you do it my way?"

He was defeated. He couldn't refuse her anything. Maybe her sense of values didn't agree with his but how many lovers agreed on everything?

One might be crazy about the color of red but the other could easily feel that blue or some other color was best. They didn't have to fight because their opinions varied. You gave as much as possible and you took what you could.

"I won't let you down," he said. "If only that Skip —"

"We need him."

"Yeah, I guess we do," Dutch admitted.

"We just have to tolerate the guy. By next year we should have a following of our own."

"Leaving out the kind of girls I've seen so far."

"Well —"

"I mean it, Cherry. That still is like holding a stick of dynamite between your teeth and hoping that you won't lose them when it goes off. As for the men — their impression of us has been nil."

"You can't please everybody."

"That's for sure."

The phone rang and he went over to answer it. This was Sunday and nobody ever called them on Sunday.

"Yeah?" he said into the phone.

"This — Dutch, this is Penny."

"Oh. Sorry you lost out for a couple of days but what could we do. The rain —"

"I know all about the rain. Honest. It's coming through the roof of the shack."

"Put a pan under the leak."

"And let it ruin my ceiling."

"You've got a point there."

"I — Dutch, I tried in town. Nobody would come out. Nobody would do anything. All it needs is a piece of tin between the shingles but I can't get up there to do it. If it isn't fixed the ceiling will be on the floor by morning."

He glanced out at rain. It was coming down harder.

"Rest easy. I'll see what I can do."

"I — gee, thanks. I hate to interrupt you and —"

"I wasn't doing much. Just bitching."

"Thanks," she said again.

He hung up and placed his glass on top of the television set.

"Penny," he said to Cherry. "Her roof is leaking."

"Let it leak."

"Why?"

"It's an excuse. She thinks that if she gets you alone —"

"She doesn't make excuses. You can't ask a woman to go out in this. Out here in the country we help each other."

"Naturally. In every way that you can. Mostly a girl only has to have one kind of help. The only method she can get it is with a man."

He walked over to her and pulled her to her feet. Her flesh was warm and naked under the dress.

"You know better than that. If I didn't have a girl who was a girl you might be right but I've got everything with you that any man could want."

She pushed in close to him.

"Love me, Dutch?"

"I keep telling you that, don't I?"

"Yes, but do you love me for what I am or because of what I do for you?"

"Because of both reasons."

She brought his head down with her hands and kissed him on the mouth.

"Is the other necessary for love?"

"It's an expression of love."

"Or a convenience."

"There are times when you could claim it was that."

"Don't stay," she whispered.

"I won't."

"And fix her roof."

"But what else."

"Honey, if you don't know I won't tell you."

He should have worn a coat but he didn't bother with one. The only actual protection against the weather was a parka that he'd used in Iceland and that was too heavy for the present climate.

Rain soaked through to his skin as he walked to a shed but he found some pieces of flat tin and returned to the car.

The road was bad, just as it was always bad during and after a storm. There were dozens of chug holes filled with water and it was impossible to tell which were the worst. He hit one that shook the car and he hoped he hadn't cracked a spring.

Penny was waiting for him when he reached the shack. He walked past her and on inside.

"This is decent of you," she said.

"At least there's something decent about me."

"There you go, twisting my words. I wish you wouldn't."

The leak was in the living room, the water splashing as it fell into the pail beneath it.

"Any space above the ceiling?" he asked. "If I haven't forgotten there is."

"Yes, but it isn't big enough for you."

"The hell."

"I've been up there twice. You get into it through a trap door in the bedroom. Then you crawl on your belly."

He looked at the white dress she was wearing. The dress had a row of gold buttons down the front and one was missing, causing the material to separate and revealing her naked skin underneath.

"You'd better do it again," he said. "Take a knife with you and when you find the leak shove it on through so I know where to put the tin."

"I expected that."

He left the shack and walked around back for a ladder. The ladder was old but he had to trust it if he was going to get up on the roof.

Once he was up on the roof he began to feel the full force of the rain. The wind had risen and it whipped the storm across the field. He waited, soaked and cold, for the appearance of the knife.

"Here," he heard her say. "See?"

He told her to remove the knife and then he shoved the piece of tin into place.

"Still leaking?" he inquired.

"No."

"So you're all set, aren't you?"

"If I can talk to you a moment before you go."

"Well —"

"Besides, I upset the chair and I can't get down through the trap door by myself."

He said nothing and descended the ladder. One of the rungs cracked, giving him a scare, and he swore. He left the ladder right where it was and re-entered the shack.

The bedroom was small and neat. He noticed the photograph of a baby on the dresser and he guessed it had been her kid. The kid didn't look like her but all kids looked alike to him.

"I'm here," he said.

Her feet and legs came into view first and he couldn't miss the fullness of her thighs as the hem of the dress caught on something and jerked itself up. He could have looked past her thighs but he didn't. He knew what she was like.

Dutch held her around the waist and brought her down to the floor, then let go.

"Thanks," she said.

"You're welcome."

She turned, facing him. Her white dress was a mess, covered with dirt. She had lost two more buttons beyond the one already missing, and she just about hung open in front. He studied her with interest. There wasn't as much to her as Cherry but she had all that she needed to be a woman.

"You're soaked," she exclaimed, concerned.

"I'll dry out."

"And get sick."

"Sick? I've never been sick. Even when I was in school and the measles were going strong I —"

"Dutch, you are sick. But you don't know it."

"Television could use that kind of a joke."

"I mean it. Sick in the head."

Disgust flooded his face.

"I fixed your damned roof. What more do you want?"

"Not what she wants."

"She? That's Cherry."

"One thing, she doesn't deserve the name."

"If you were a man I'd slug you for that remark."

"So that you could try and prove that you're never wrong? That's very funny, Dutch. You're as blind as a bat in the sun. You're as dumb as a fellow on his first date."

"My first date was with you."

"Yes. To the movies."

"So I wasted a couple of bucks."

"Why? Because we held hands? And after that, a night or so — well, how does a girl ask? You see sex at home and you don't know what it's all about. It's theirs, their right, but it doesn't belong to you. You ask a question and somebody just shrugs. You might as well talk to a stone in the middle of a field. You have the feelings but you don't know just what they are. Then, like me, you get a night when you feel that nothing is important, that the reality of life will never belong to you. You take a drink to be one of the gang. Then you drink more because it isn't so bad. After that —"

"Yeah. After that. Who cares? I don't, not right now. I'm wet and cold. Your roof is okay."

"Cold?" Penny laughed. "She'll warm you up."

His fists clenched.

"Shut your face."

"I won't and you can't make me. Isn't one of us enough for you? Or do you have to make her the same way?"

He turned from Penny.

"I'm going," he said. "If you get another leak throw a match to the shack."

"This is my home."

"Don't brag. It's some home."

She followed him out to the living room. It was fine with her but he didn't need Penny. All he had to have was up at the house. Cherry was for him. Cherry. Cherry, dark and lovely, seeking the world. Cherry who loved blindly and with passion. Cherry who would bear his children, love him always. It didn't matter that he couldn't believe in what they were doing. All that mattered to him was what they meant to each other.

"I'm looking for a job," Penny said.

He paused in the middle of the living room.

"Luck," he told her.

"Don't you care?"

"Should I?"

"You did once."

"That was once." A chill shook him and he moved close to the oil burner that was running, putting his back to it. The heat felt fine. "Once," he repeated.

"A job," she went on. "In a diner. The pay is nothing but they say the tips are good. There was an opening in a restaurant, too, but I couldn't consider it. When you work in a restaurant you have to carry heavy trays and I won't be able to do that later on. The diner sells mostly sandwiches and coffee and I can stay at that until it's time for me —"

"Hey, you're not even sure."

"I hope it's true."

"Your trolley just went off the track and down the bank. What girl would want —"

"Me. I'm scared but that's what I want. We'll never have anything else together, because of her, but this part of us I can always keep. It won't be like before, the drinking and the helling around. I'll get rid of the shack and move somewhere else, pretend that I'm a widow or divorced. Others have done the same thing. They — Dutch, you're terribly wet."

"Yeah. The heat is okay."

She stood there and he couldn't look at her. She had courage in depth, a courage that reached out to him and which, in self defense and inner confusion, he attempted to reject. Courage? No, more than that. Guts. Guts to meet the world on unequal terms, to rear a child without a father, to hold her head high while struggling against the conventions of society.

"This is a hell of a thing," he said.

"No. It's a beautiful thing. It's all of the love that I can have from you, the only real thing that you can give me."

His wet clothes began to steam and he moved away from the stove. He felt uncomfortable, as though he wanted to run and he couldn't. When you ran you left your past behind you but the memories of what you had done kept crashing into your skull.

"I'd like you to stay on at the farm," he said.

"So I can show myself to those men."

"It's not what you think."

"No. It's worse. Nobody has to tell me why they are there, or the truth about the girls. And that Skip Bart — well, he got his picture of me. He —"

"The hell he did!"

"Yes. At the stand. From the waist up. How could I —"

"Cripes. I'll ram that camera down his throat."

"Get my picture back."

"You can bet that I will."

She touched one of his arms with her hand. Her fingers moved, digging in. She did that sometimes, as though she were trying to find an object to which she could cling.

"You're shaking," she said.

"Yeah. That rain, it goes past your skin and all the way inside."

"I've got hangers. You could take off your clothes and dry them. If they're hung over the burner it won't take long."

He laughed, a raged, almost lonely laugh.

"What are you looking for? A cheap thrill?"

"You don't mind when you're up on the farm when the others are there. You don't mind with her."

"That's another type of situation."

Her fingernails sank as far as they could go into his arm and he felt the pain. She was strong, a hill girl. Her muscles didn't show but she could plow the land or swing an axe. He'd seen her do both, then experienced the female loveliness of her as he'd taken her into his arms.

"And this is a different situation," she said. "I'll go along on the idea that the farm is another type."

He looked down at the arm she was holding and then at her. Beyond the opening of her dress she was naked, her skin smooth and white. She didn't get any sun in the stand and when she wasn't busy she didn't walk around outside.

"Your dress is filthy," he told her.

"Naturally. There's just a little space up there. I said you had to crawl on your belly and you do. When I went up there before it was to get away from Cliff. That was before the baby was born and I was so fat I couldn't move much. He'd get drunk and beat me and I didn't know what harm he'd do. Then he'd sit by the door and fall asleep. When he woke up he was insane. There was no other place for me to go."

He could just about see her, struggling through the opening in the ceiling, hiding, afraid for herself and her unborn child. A love child. A — no, not that. Not a love child. A child of passion. A love child was born from love. A child of passion was a mistake.

Breathing heavily, he reached for one of the buttons on her dress. Her fingers bored into his other arm, her nails almost cutting through the skin. If she had a child by him it would be neither a love child or a passion child. Something that only a man who was a savage could possibly give her. A revenge child.

"It won't unbutton," he said.

"You can't unbutton that one."

"Why?"

"The rest are just sewed on. The top ones only unbutton so you can get out of the thing." She smiled up at him. "Don't be so stupid, Dutch. What you put on you have to take off."

"Yeah."

"I'd feel better if you were out of those wet clothes."

"And I'd feel a whole lot better if you were out of that dress."

"So you can have with me what you have with her?"

"Aw, you spoil everything."

"I'm not one of those bums from the city."

"They're bums all right."

She let go of his arm.

"Yes," she said. "Girls without love or the ability to love. Girls wandering, no purpose or decency in their lives. They think no more of having an abortion than getting a cold in their heads."

"Well, there may be times when — "

"There's never a time for that. There — "

She turned and walked into the bedroom. He shrugged and removed his wet shirt. Cherry was waiting for him, no doubt wanting what he wanted. He shrugged again and moved toward the door.

"So long," he shouted.

He didn't wait for a reply but stepped outside into the rain that lashed at him in fury.

There was no more revenge to be had from her. He had taken it all.

It was, to put it mildly, a hollow victory.

9

THE RAIN CONTINUED until Thursday and they played cards and drank most of the time. They sat at the kitchen table, the gas burners of the stove on, making it too hot and yet it was chilly when the burners were turned off. Generally they were naked, living in a world apart from reality, living in a world that wasn't actually a world at all.

"Wrong card," she said. "You had a king. Why didn't you play it?"

He threw the cards aside.

"I'm sick of this," he decided.

"Of me?"

"No. This. Of course I'm not sick of you. Hell."

She laughed.

"I didn't really think you were sick of me. Anyway I haven't noticed it upstairs."

"It's this doing nothing. A man should have a job. A man is supposed to work. What can he hope to get if he doesn't?"

"Be patient until September. Then we can count our money. I'll stuff a mattress with it and give birth to five dollar bills."

"Yeah, bills that we've got to pay."

"Who worries over them when you've got the cash."

He got the last two cans of beer from the refrigerator. There was a box full of empties outside and he hadn't been into town to get any liquor.

"I'm going to sell the place," he said as he poured for her.

"Get your head examined first."

"For what? I'm serious. I don't need a mattress stuffed with money. All I need is you and to get out of here. This is the time of the year to unload a spot in the country. This — "

"Yes?"

He sat down heavily. He couldn't carry what was inside of him alone any longer. The days made weeks and the weeks made months. Nine months made a baby.

"The blonde," he said and hesitated. He looked at his beer. "Yeah, the blonde."

"She's nobody."

"Everybody is somebody."

"I'm upset. She got a job, didn't she?"

"In a diner."

"Small loss, big gain. Some girls go for this and some don't. She didn't. Too nice, that shack bitch."

He continued to look at his beer.

"She may have a baby," he said.

"How clever of her. I suppose one of these farm hands — "

"No. Not one of them. It's mine."

There was a long silence.

"Yours?" Cherry didn't seem to be bitter or alarmed.

"I'm afraid so. She don't know for sure just yet but if she is that way I'm the guy."

"Let her prove it."

"No. I meet my obligations. I only thought you should know. Even after we're married the dough has to go out for the kid every month. It'll be a hole out of whatever we have but I'm as much to blame as she is — perhaps more. She believed that I was honest and I only wanted her in one way."

"The same as you want me?"

"No."

"You're lying."

His eyes locked with hers, held.

"That's not a nice thing to say."

"Maybe not. I'm — sorry."

"Figure the total, Cherry. I went all out for you and I held nothing in. Money that I should have saved — we should have saved — I've tossed away on this farm. We won't get it back but we can make the break. Read the stuff you've got. There's no fortune to be made in a straight nudist camp business. Those people are dedicated and I'm not. I'm anxious to make money but I've decided that I won't do it with loose girls and lonely men. To do this right would take years of near poverty. I can't wait and I won't wait."

"Go on," she said when he stopped.

He drank some of the beer. He wished he had more. He needed more because all of this was coming out and he wasn't quite sure how to say it. Yet he had to say what he felt, to open the faucet of his emotions and let them run wild. When he had her body everything was right, nothing impossible, but once he had exhausted himself with her favors all of the fears he had ever known nagged at him, cut through his brain like a knife, except the cut was deeper than a knife would have made it.

"You're not with me," he said. "You're — " She laughed.

"I've been with you."

"No, not that. You've got your eyes of gold and I haven't. I've never been hungry for money. Sure. I want things the same as anybody else but I won't sell my soul to pay for them. The money I had was an accident. I didn't plan on saving anything. It was just that my pay was good and I had no way of spending it up there. I went there to get away from her. From the blonde. Penny. I've told you how it was, haven't I? Yeah. Some but it doesn't matter. There's you and me now and that's what matters. We don't need the world. We just need each other and a chance. We — "

"You have to be practical," she said. She rubbed one of her naked breasts with her hand. "Right now we need something to drink. You can't sit out here in this rain and not drink. As soon as it stops we'll be busy. Why not enjoy ourselves while we can? When it gets to be September we'll know whether or not we're right for each other."

"September," he repeated. He was disgusted, not because of her but because he somehow couldn't project all that he believed. "Yeah, naturally. September."

She reached across the table and took one of his hands in hers. She held it, looking down, parting his fingers as though she was counting them.

"Look, Dutch." She lifted her eyes to his face. "Will you look and understand? Will you look at me and try and understand what I am? Beautiful? They say so. Men before you have told me that. I — well, I wasn't any virgin when we met. I didn't expect that I would be when I met the man I loved or that he would find it necessary for me to be one. There was the poverty at home, money as scarce as Santa Claus on the

Fourth of July, but my face and shape got me dates with fellows who could afford to show me a good time. A few of them were decent, content to be out with a pretty girl, but there were others who had to be pleased."

"Damn," he said, not wanting to know this because it would hurt, yet wanting to know the truth.

She appeared to be counting his fingers again. Her breathing was unsteady, her breasts rising and falling as she breathed.

"A girl paid back home," Cherry said. "She paid the fellow or she stayed inside the house and listened to her father and mother, both drunk, fighting over money. I told myself then that I would never fight for it, not with somebody else, but that I'd go out and get it. I was sick after I got to the city — the men wanted the same thing there as those in the town I had left — but I had a chance to pose and use just my figure and get paid for it. But I tired of that, too. There was no future to it, just an end. When I met you I was ready for love, to be loved. You had this place and I knew something about being a nudist. I also knew that we couldn't hope to make a fortune if we were legitimate — just as you said you'd read that we couldn't. This, what we're doing, is the only answer. There's no other way."

"All of which has nothing to do with us as a couple."

Her eyes told him that he was being impossible.

"It does, Dutch. Terribly. Do you want us to have a kid and see the kid go without shoes? I don't. I must have been four or five before I had a pair. I won't wish that on a child of my own. I—yes, you probably could make fairly big money if you were working. But how long can you keep it up? All your life or until you retire? And what would we have then? A hole in the wall where the furnace won't work? Please, Dutch, don't ask me to go through that. What we're doing isn't wrong. It's the people who come here who are wrong. They aren't our responsibility. If a girl has found what she thinks to be an easy dollar and a man is willing to give it to her it's no business of ours. What they do here they could do almost anywhere else. As long as what we have between us is clean we don't have to worry about anybody at all."

"Okay," he said, giving up and removing his hand from hers. "I'll go along with what you want but why do we have to wait until September?"

"For a very good reason. You may be tired of me by then."

"I'll never get tired of you," Dutch promised. "I didn't jump into this with my eyes closed." He wondered if he hadn't. "You had an idea and I bought it. I — "

"You're sweet." The softness in her voice clawed at him.

"But not sweet enough to —"

"I want to be sure and I want you to be sure." She got up from the table. "Settling for less is stupid."

"About Penny's kid — "

"That was an accident. How many of us would be alive today if we weren't accidents?"

"You don't hate me?"

She stood there, nude and smiling.

"Of course not."

"Now you're the one who's sweet."

"Well — "

"If you want to go out into the rain."

She was delightful, inviting, but he tore himself away from her to go upstairs and dress. When he came down she was drinking the beer that he had left in his can.

"We could use the blonde at the snack stand," she said as he kissed her before going. "I won't have time to do the work and you'd find it boring. If you talked to her she might change her mind."

"I doubt it."

Cherry nodded.

"I suppose that's so. Anyway, forget that I even mentioned the thing."

But as he drove toward Cranston he didn't forget about it. Penny's shack looked pitifully unattractive, deserted. With the coming of a kid she'd be unable to put on a new siding and roof. She'd live there as a forgotten woman. And it was his fault. Maybe it had been his fault from the beginning. He'd had honor then, perhaps too much of it. What about those couple of nights, frustrated and uncertain of himself, when he'd brought her near total surrender, had heard her mild objections and then retreated? Wouldn't any moral girl refuse and pretend? If she was in love wasn't she as anxious to express her love as the man? Of course, only man is the aggressive force. So he had aroused her, perhaps, and done nothing about it. Then that one Saturday night with Cliff — it could happen to any girl, couldn't it?

He lit a cigarette and turned onto the highway. He saw the bitterness that had caused him to go away as a mask behind which he had hid. Actually, her becoming pregnant by Cliff had been more shock than bitterness. Still he hadn't recognized that. He'd returned home and he'd done this to her. Who had he really hurt? The child to be born far greater than anybody else. She'd suffer and he'd feel the guilt but the child was the one who would always carry their shame.

September ...

Months ahead but after that he'd have the girl he loved. Cherry understood what he had done and he'd pay for his love child. They'd marry and move on, shutting out as much of the past as possible. He would sleep with his head upon her breasts, her body naked and coming alive during the night. Her lips over his mouth would awaken him, pleading silently, and their love would grow with each new and wonderful experience.

Once he reached town he picked up the liquor and beer, thought about it for a moment and stopped off at the diner where Penny had taken a job.

She was alone, killing time in back of the counter. The white uniform was too small for her, the material firm and rounded over her breasts.

"There are other diners," she said coldly

He sat down on a stool.

"Maybe I like this one."

"And maybe I'd like to forget."

"Do you think that's possible?"

She drew a cup of coffee for him.

"I can try." She put the cup in front of him and stared out at the rain. "It won't be the first thing that I've had to forget."

He stirred the coffee. Tragedy, she had lived it and she was going through it again. This time there would be no husband, no beatings, just a child to constantly remind her that her tragedy was complete.

"I didn't see your car anywhere around," he said.

She shrugged.

"You won't. Something went wrong with the motor." Her voice remained cold. "Everything has gone wrong."

Her last remark was so true that it required no comment.

"How do you get to work?"

"Do you care?"

"Would I ask, if I wasn't?"

"I don't know. I hire a cab."

"That's pretty expensive."

"It doesn't pay in this weather." Her next shrug was more pronounced. "But the summer should be good, or the weekend if it clears, and I've got to hang on."

"There's the stand —"

"Thanks for nothing. I'll stay dressed while I'm on the job."

He studied the menu over the grill. It was the usual thing for a diner.

"Suit yourself," he said.

"Don't worry. I will." Her eyes focused on his face, searching. "They're talking about you, Dutch."

"Who's talking?"

"Lots of people."

"How would they know anything about me?"

"Aren't you smart?"

"Sometimes. Sometimes not."

She glanced at the clock.

"It started with a man who did printing for you and you shouldn't have to be told that folks are interested in whatever is sensational."

Dutch swore. People just couldn't do a job and keep their mouths shut. They had to run off at the mouth and the further the gossip went the worse it got. Everybody had to add their own impressions.

"To hell with them," he said. "I own the land and I pay my taxes."

"Yes, and you'll probably pay a fine."

"For what?"

"For being dumb."

Thoughtfully, he drank his coffee. Dumb? Possibly. But he was in love and that made a difference.

"What time do you finish work?" he asked.

"I am finished. I'm only waiting for my relief."

"Then you can ride in with me."

"And make Cherry angry?"

"She knows about us."

Penny's eyebrows arched.

"About me being —"

"Yes."

"She must have really blown up."

"No. She was more than decent about it."

More friendly now, perhaps sensing that he had been a man about his mistake, she started to pick up his cup for a refill. Not wanting any, he caught her hand and held it.

"She's regular," he insisted.

"I'm glad you think so."

"Well, it would be too much to expect you to agree."

"How can I? I'm a girl and I know how a girl reacts when she's faced with that kind of a situation. Her love would have to be blind to make her want to have anything to do with it. Cherry's love isn't that strong. She's as weak as they come and some of them come pretty weak."

He let go of her hand. He wished that he hadn't entered the diner. All they could do was hurt each other and there was no point in that. Nobody chopped down a tree just to see it fall.

Still —

He stayed with her until her relief arrived and then he made her come with him. She refused at first and they fought about it but she finally consented.

She got soaked as they ran through the rain to the car and the uniform stuck to her all over.

"I'm sorry," she said after they had gone a couple of blocks.

"Who isn't?"

"I mean being nasty to you."

"I'd say it was pretty human for a girl to be nasty under the circumstances. You've got our mistake inside of you and I'm going to marry another girl. Why wouldn't you be nasty?"

"It solves nothing."

"No."

"And she'll solve nothing for you."

Dutch stopped for a red light.

"Drop it about her," he said. "Let's talk about you. I used to be sore but I'm not sore any longer. Your penalty for going out with Cliff was more than it should have been."

She moved close to him as they crossed the intersection.

"Dutch," she said quietly. "Dutch we can make it right."

"Huh?"

"It's the only decent thing to do. Maybe you don't love me now but you might later on. She walked into your life with a sensational body and that's all she's got. I've got a body that isn't so bad. I know most men want that and yet it isn't what is most important. If you marry her for that alone you'll be sorry. Marry me for our child and I'll make you happy."

He considered it lightly for a moment.

"No," he said firmly. "It has to go beyond that, Penny. I'll send support money and keep my word. It's a rugged deal for you but I can't help that now. We have to live with what we did."

Defeated, she slid across the seat away from him.

"Then I think I should show you something."

"Whatever you've got I've already seen."

"I'm afraid that isn't true."

"So I'll listen."

"People are talking about both of us."

"Go on."

"I told myself that I could take it, that I could live it down, but there is a limit to what one person can do alone. When you came into the diner I thought you knew but it didn't follow that you would have bothered with me if you'd known. I — well, when you're desperate you sometimes try to hate people that you really love. I— Dutch, I'm not making very much sense, am I?"

"You lost me in a hurry," he admitted.

"Wait until we get to the shack."

"Sure. I've got no other choice."

The rain began to let up and the sky seemed brighter. If the sun came out hot for the weekend the farm would be crawling with nude people. He grunted his disgust for what the guests would do. However, when you needed money you needed it. To deny that was to be ignorant.

He found the shack warm when they went inside.

"I hope this weather lets up," she said. "I'm almost out of oil."

"I've got some dough for you."

"Thanks, but you've given me enough already."

"Yeah, I guess I did."

She went into the bedroom but he didn't follow her. He felt no urge to do that. Cherry was at the farm and they'd drink and make love.

He was sitting on the sofa when she came out of the bedroom.

"Hey," he said. "You nuts or something?"

She had shrugged out of the top part of her uniform and she was naked to the waist, her bare breasts tempting and proud.

"Other men like me this way," she said.

"Why wouldn't they if you gave them the opportunity to look?"

"They're looking."

"That's your affair."

She walked over to him.

"They're looking at this."

She shoved a picture into his hand and he examined it. The picture was of Penny, taken while she was working at the stand up on the farm.

"I don't get the drift of the whole thing," he said slowly. "I knew there was a picture taken but I don't see where this print came from."

"A lot of copies have been sold in town. This one some sneering crumb gave me in the diner. He said if I'd do this I'd do anything."

"The hell," Dutch said savagely. "This was none of my doings."

"I'm positive it wasn't. In the beginning I did wonder but I couldn't imagine a man who had slept with a girl being that low."

"It's Skip Bart," he decided.

"Yes, it would be like him. Or her."

"Shut up."

"I won't. It was somebody and that's all I know. How do you think I feel? This is my home and the people know me. I — Dutch, I said the car wouldn't run but that was a lie. I sold it for what I could get. Look behind the shack if you don't believe me. I sold it so I would have some money to get away from here but once I had the money I realized that you can never run away completely. And what good would it do to me to run? I'd only be able to work a few lousy months and then I'd find myself helpless amongst a bunch of strangers."

Dutch cursed and tore the photo in small pieces. He dropped the pieces onto the floor and got up from the sofa.

"I'll kill the slob," he said violently. "When I hit him he'll think he ran straight into a truck."

She grabbed him before he opened the door.

"Please, Dutch," she begged and tugged at his arm. "We're both in a mess but don't make it worse by losing your temper." She came up against him, hard and furious. "Just lose yourself with me. For now and tonight. For always. For what may be the last time we'll ever know together."

"I'm no pig," he said and shoved her away from him.

Still cursing he opened the door and walked outside.

The rain had stopped but he didn't notice it. Something was wrong. All the way wrong.

10

ALL OF IT, when he considered what Cherry said, sounded logical enough. Penny, regardless of the love she claimed to have for him, was bitter and out to destroy him.

"It's a pattern," Cherry declared. "A pattern of jealousy that's as wicked as any sin. And more ruthless. You're mine and she wants you so she'd even degrade herself to bring the police out here."

"Cripes. The female mind. How does a man keep up with it?"

She came to him in the darkness of the night.

"He doesn't, Dutch. He pleases her physically and he doesn't worry about the rest of it."

His mouth mashed her lips while his hands roamed her loveliness.

"I suppose you want to be pleased?"

"That's the general idea."

He didn't get much sleep that night and the next morning he was tired. The day was clear, nice and hot, and while she stayed in the house to answer the phone he did what had to be done outside. He emptied the boats, straightened up things in the barn and checked the snack stand for supplies. By noon the grass was dry.

"We're filling up," she said with a smile when he returned to the house.

"With the usual girls, I suppose?"

"Be practical, Dutch. What would a man do up here in the country without a girl?"

"Enjoy the sun."

"Do you think the sun is more fun?"

"I didn't say that."

"The nights are better."

"Ours are anyway."

She laughed as he kissed her.

"Eight nights a week," she said. "You count last night as two."

They needed a few things from town and she drove in to get them. It was impossible for them to go together because of the phone and she claimed she got lonely in the house when she was by herself.

He sat at the kitchen table, drinking beer and thinking about Penny. If she was intent upon betraying him she had the power to do it. Or at least she could come close. One was almost as bad as the other.

About three the phone rang and he answered it.

"Remember me?" the man asked.

"How could I? I don't recognize your voice and I can't see you."

"I'm the fat man. The one with the Caddy. I was up there to look at your place."

"Yes, I remember now."

"Got a room available?"

"I think so."

"And a girl?"

"That's up to you. There'll be some here but you're on your own. You don't get a girl with the room."

"The photographer fellow said some of them came high."

"I wouldn't know."

"You're no help so I'll take my own chances. Save me a room."

"Sure."

He got a few more reservations after that from men on the prowl and Skip Bart phoned.

"I'll be on the evening bus. Meet me?"

"I'll think about it."

"Fine but don't strain yourself."

"I won't."

Cherry arrived at five and he unloaded the car, piling the stuff on the back porch.

"That town stinks," she said.

"It's just a town. There are thousands just like it. The people crawl through their lives and die broke."

"We won't. Just follow me."

"What do you think I've been doing?"

Some of the guests began driving in after that. Cherry understood the procedure better than he did and he left the details up to her. She signed the men and girls in — the girls came up in a couple of cars by themselves — collected the fees and took care of placing the sex hunters in the house or the barn.

When he left for town to pick up Skip he couldn't find her since she was off with somebody and he wrote a note, placing it on the kitchen table.

Outside, walking toward his car, he met the girl who had stayed with him that first night in the city. She had already gotten out of her clothes but her figure didn't interest him in the least.

"I should ask for change," he told her. "Maybe I should even ask for a refund."

"Try and get it. What you bought was like booze. Once it's gone there's no more left."

"All right. I'll settle for an answer to a question."

"You can ask it, guy, but I don't know whether I've got two left feet or none."

"Well, rest easy on one thing. You haven't got any brains."

"Who pays for brains?"

"You'd be surprised."

"Would I? You may be surprised yourself."

It wasn't much of a remark but it made him think on the way into Cranston. He tried to add the recent events together and come to a conclusion — but came out with nothing. A blank. An empty hole. Yet certain obscure facts were there and while he was aware they were present he was totally unable to arrange them in a proper sequence.

"Shoot square," his father had told him. "When you hit the middle go the distance but don't cross the white lines or go against your better judgement."

He shook his head.

He didn't know.

He simply didn't.

As usual, the bus was late. Skip Bart got off, carrying his equipment and walked over to the car.

"Filled up, aren't you?" he asked.

"I doubt that."

Skip put his things on the back seat and got in.

"But a good crowd?"

"This is some clunker," he said.

"You're willing to ride in it."

"Saves cab fare."

"Swell. The next time you walk."

Dutch pushed the Ford through traffic.

"You did a stupid thing," he said to Skip.

"Plenty of people are stupid. You get the habit and you can't shake it."

"Yes, but you shouldn't have let go of that photo of Penny."

"The girl who works the stand?"

"She did. Not any more. And she's the one I mean. That picture is floating around town and I don't like it. Not to mention how she feels about that, why — "

"That rotten scum!" Skip almost shouted. "He said — "

"What did he say?" Dutch's voice was tight.

"Never mind."

"I'll mind all I want."

"Hot for the girl, huh?"

"Look — "

"Wrestle her down onto a mattress and she'd be okay."

They were outside of town, in the country.

"I'll find out," Dutch said firmly.

"Aw, what's the odds? The man lied to me but he isn't the first one who's done that."

When they were opposite a gravel bank Dutch pulled the car off the road and drifted to a halt. He'd killed a snake in there once and he compared Skip to the snake. From what he knew he found the snake to be more human. This man, without morals, ate off of the flesh of others. The flesh of girls, using them for his own profit.

"Say," Skip exclaimed, looking around anxiously.

"Say, fellow, I don't like this."

"Crap. You're just yellow."

"Yellow? Hardly only I should be up at the farm."

"You'll get there — in one or a dozen pieces. You'll — understand this, will you? Traffic's light on this road and I can bust you silly before the next driver can change gears. I've got the feeling that Penny didn't have anything to do with this, or that if she did it was entirely innocent on her part. Last night I could accept the thought that she was trying to hurt me but there isn't any solid reason for that. You see things more calmly when you study them." He paused. "I've studied you, Skip. I dislike your guts — hate what's inside of you — and I'd just as soon spill them out there on the ground as I would spit in your face. Spill your guts and stomp on them. Don't for one second hope that I won't. Don't — the picture, fellow. You took it and you did something with it. Just what did you do? I'm hearing you and you're talking."

There was fear in Skip's face. It was white, his eyes reflecting his fear. He swallowed with difficulty.

"She's only some fast fun for you," he said. "So you can jolt her and then she becomes a queen. You —"

Dutch's fist was fast and deadly. Because he was sitting down he couldn't power it with everything he had but Skip's head snapped to the side.

"Don't toy with me," Dutch said.

Skip rubbed at the spot where he'd been struck.

"Nuts to it," he mumbled. "What does all of this prove?"

"Try me and learn for yourself."

"It wasn't my fault."

"So whose fault was it?"

"Some jerk's fault. He — well, okay. I take pictures at the camp, don't I?"

"Yes, and I don't think you should."

"Some people want them."

"What for?"

"You've got me. A picture has to be developed, doesn't it?"

"With most cameras."

"All right. I don't have the equipment up here for that. My error but I don't have a big operation. In the city I could do it but not up here. So I need a local guy, don't I?"

"If there's one who's willing."

"Yeah, and that's the trouble. The big shops don't want the junk in their places. It has to be a little guy, doesn't it? A hungry guy?"

"Probably."

"I found one in town. He charges the hell out of me but what can I do? I could use the pictures during the next couple of weeks or months but when you're chasing a buck you don't wait. You can't wait. Nobody can wait."

"Drop dead or make sense," Dutch said. His tone held the threat of more violence in it. He was plowing for facts and he wouldn't accept anything less. "I haven't got much patience," he went on.

"Sometimes I don't even know what the word means."

"Hell, I'm trying to tell you, ain't I?" Skip protested.

"Then do it."

"I — okay. This guy works out of his home, got a shop in the cellar, so a dollar looks big to him. Something about a mortgage and a slut for a wife. I don't know and I don't care. He was in the phone book and I finally found him. In a bar, sitting there, doing nothing. I gave him a pitch and we made a deal. I said his price was high and that's no lie. But I couldn't help that. The bad thing is he gets it into his head that he should make up some prints and ship them into the city, selling them. This I can't and I wouldn't do. Not until he came across the one of Penny. He swore he'd sell the photo out of town and I couldn't see any harm in it. Keep him happy, you know? She was mad when I took the picture and she meant nothing to me. What dame ever did? They're all the same, born with empty pocketbooks and doing anything to fill them up." Skip wiped off his mouth with the back of one hand, then fingered the spot where Dutch had struck him. "Let's go out to the farm, huh? You wanted to know and now you know. Don't park off the garbage of what he did in my yard. I suppose he was after money and he got his easy by selling a picture of a local girl with nice bouncers. He shouldn't have done it but he did. It's not good for either one of us but we both understand that you can never take anything back."

Dutch didn't throw up but he felt sick as the weight of what had been done to Penny splashed down into his stomach like a rock.

"We'll have some new rules," he said as he swung the car out onto the road.

"Such as what?"

"Such as no pictures. When Cherry talked to me about this she said the people wanted privacy. What kind of privacy do they have when you're running around with a camera?"

"Whose business is it?"

"Mine. I own the property. I'm responsible for what happens. There's enough gossip about a nudist camp in town without adding to it."

"You'd better get smart," Skip said.

"Don't tell me what to do. I am getting smart."

"Look, Dutch. Why fight? You're taking in your fees and I earn what I can. We've all got bills to pay, haven't we?"

"True. But what I make is spent almost before I can count it."

"Is that my affair?"

"No."

Dutch made the turn off onto the mountain road.

"The fat guy with the Caddy get here?" Skip inquired.

"If he did it was after I left."

"He's a hog, fellow. I could have gotten him a girl in the city but he has to have the best. Yeah, the best. So much woman that she'll make him feel like twenty again. These creeps give me a pain. Rich bastards, filthy with money. Most of them think they can buy anything and generally they get their wish."

Dutch dug for a cigarette, found only one that was broken and threw it outside. A litter-bug, he thought. Funny, wasn't it, that he should remind himself of this just then? He had bigger problems than that.

"Put your camera up for the weekend," he said. "If that fellow ever spread those pictures around we'd be ruined."

Skip laughed.

"Maybe you can't tell me what to do. Ever consider that?"

"Why should I? The farm is mine. You haven't got a lease on one foot of it."

"I don't need any lease." Skip laughed again. "You're in a bad way, guy, and you don't know it."

"If you don't shut up you'll be in a bad way."

"I wouldn't count on it."

When he drove past Penny's shack he felt a terrible sense of shame and guilt. Not only was she suffering with the knowledge that she would bear his child but that picture had degraded her in the town. She'd become the subject of the depraved wishes of men in bars and garages and on the street corners.

"I'll belt that photographer," he said thickly. "Not the way I did with you. Hard. So they have to put his jaw together with pieces of wire."

"Where would it get you?"

Dutch said nothing in reply. It was a good question and the answer to it escaped him. He just knew that a great harm had been done. That he had a great sympathy for Penny and that more was taking place on the farm than he realized. There was one thing that was important — why didn't the men who stayed for a weekend never return? Certainly it wasn't because the girls weren't beautiful. They were. Young, their bodies glistening in the sun. No man could ask for more and yet something was lacking. The camp fees, were they responsible? Possibly. They were very high in comparison to the fees charged by other camps he had read about. While the men were important and had money that could bother them. Probably after they stayed at the farm they came to the conclusion that what they received wasn't worth the cost. There were any number of girls in the city who had their own apartments and charged modest rates for their favors.

"You'd better turn the camera over to me," Dutch said.

"Why don't we talk to Cherry first?"

"I doubt if she approves."

"There's only one way to find out. Ask."

"I will."

He drove into the lane. More cars had arrived since he had left for the bus station and they were parked all over the lawn. He saw the fat man's Caddy but it wasn't the only Caddy on the grounds. All of the other cars were big, most of them new, and he had difficulty finding a spot for the Ford.

Some of the guests were down near the lake, a couple were in swimming — the water would be cold after so much rain — and Cherry stood near the porch talking to the fat man. Obviously the fat man had just reached the farm because he was still dressed. However, Cherry had shed her clothes and she was a nude dream of female flesh. Dutch thirsted and longed for her in a sudden wave of desire. He pushed the car door open and knew that his thirst would have to wait, that his longing would be satisfied in the darkness of the night.

Skip went into the kitchen with him and put his equipment in one corner. He didn't ask for beer but crossed to the refrigerator to get a can.

"You've got some nerve," Dutch declared, resentful. "You walk in here and take what you want."

"Any reason that I shouldn't? We share, don't we?"

"I couldn't say as to that but whatever we share is nothing more than dirty money."

"Cut out being so moral."

Dutch joined Skip at the kitchen table. He stared across at the fellow, noticed the slight bruise that was beginning to show on Skip's face.

They were still sitting there when Cherry came in. Her face was flushed, her body proud and it irked him that Skip should be able to look at her when he believed that right belonged only to him.

"Level this guy off," Skip said to her. "He's beating his teeth together, telling me I should ditch my camera. Am I supposed to come up here for my health?"

Cherry moved over next to Dutch, tilted his head and kissed him on the mouth.

"Honey," she said. "Honey, don't be a prude."

"I'm not. I just don't like it. I've read a little. The majority of nudist camps don't even allow cameras."

"This is different."

Her nakedness was warm, close.

"I don't know why it should be."

She sighed.

"All right. But let him use it this weekend."

"No."

There was a long silence in the kitchen.

"I said to level him off," Skip reminded her and got up from the table. "Square him down and show him where the target is." He gave her a rough look. "I warned you about doing it before. What's the matter? You been having so much fun in bed that you can't think."

"Skip —"

"Hell, it's your job. Take care of it. If you don't —"

"Yes," she cut in wearily. "I know without you making a speech."

Skip picked up his equipment and left the kitchen. Dutch watched Cherry as she got beer for them, rinsed the glasses in cold water and then poured. She poured a lousy beer. There was never any head on it but when it came to liquor she was playing in her own field.

"You're hiding something," he said.

She made him shift his chair so she could sit down on his lap. Without thinking, his arm went around her and his hand rested gently over one breast.

"Honey, a girl always has things to hide."

"If she's in love?"

"Maybe she wouldn't be loved if she didn't."

He tasted his beer. Somehow it didn't taste right.

"I've been honest with you," he said.

"Did I insist?"

"Not exactly but I thought it was only fair. You wouldn't want me to marry you and then give you the sorry news that I'm the father of another girl's child."

She put her beer upon the table and kissed him wildly, clinging to him the way she did when they were upstairs in the room.

"Don't you trust me?" she asked.

"That isn't the thing. I trust you but I want the truth. The truth is part of being in love, isn't it?"

"Yes, only I should think you could accept me for what I am."

"I can accept you but not Skip. He's got the mind of a spider after a fly."

"He's dangerous."

"I can also accept danger. You might not think so but you live with it constantly."

She kissed him with even greater fury than before. He could almost forget about everything as he tasted her lips, felt them move against his mouth. He crushed her to him, wanting her, needing her, wanting her not only for what she was physically but because of what he told himself she was as a person.

"He's got me held down by a lever," she confided.

"I'll break the damned lever. You show me the handle and I'll smash it over his skull."

Cherry shook her head.

"You can't. Nobody can. And it isn't just one lever he has. It's two."

"Yeah?"

"The second one is you and me."

"How is that?"

"We're living together, aren't we?"

"That's our business."

Her breast rose against the cup of his hand.

"Not exactly, Dutch. There are laws."

"If you're in love with somebody?"

"A law about taking a woman across a state line for purposes that aren't moral."

"I didn't bring you up here. You came by yourself."

"Yes, I know that but what if he used the other lever on me, the one that could crush all that we've got? I love you — awfully, Dutch — and I don't want to lose you. You — well, you don't know, Skip. You just don't know him. There — Dutch, he had some pictures of me. I was drunk at the time and I didn't realize what I was doing. If he can use his camera this weekend he'll give them to me. They belong to my past and not to our future. It's all I ask of you. If you try to stop him — Dutch, I couldn't let those pictures get out. I'd be ruined and I'd lose you, no matter what I did. He'd force me to tell the police that I did come here with you, not later, that I was confused and what you've done to me was without my consent. He'd —"

"Don't you love me?" he demanded.

"Honey, I love you." She kissed him on the neck with her wet lips. "Love is strong but there are some things that are stronger. Everybody fights to be decent, don't they? I think most people do. I'll show you the pictures when I get them. There's no need for any complications. You'll have to judge me then and it's a risk I'll have to take. Let him have his way this weekend and we'll never see him again. We can change the policy of the camp and make it what it should be if it pleases you. The money we could earn means a great deal to me, to both of us, but not as much as your love. I told you it was all that I asked, that you don't stop him. On Monday, after you've seen the pictures, you'll either kick me off the farm or we'll go find somebody who can marry us."

"I suppose that's so."

"And he carries a gun."

"His type would."

"Don't be foolish enough to believe that he'd refuse to use it."

"I'm not."

A few minutes later he sat alone in the kitchen and toyed with a fresh beer. He didn't drink the beer, just sat very still and stared at the opposite wall. Actually, he should be at the snack stand, taking care of it, but he wasn't in the mood. He had gained some respect for the nudist movement, could appreciate the values, very clean, which they sought in the sun but what was taking place on the farm disturbed him. This wasn't the nudist movement as such. This was simply the oldest profession in a new atmosphere.

Presently he arose from the chair, crossed to the sink and poured out the beer.

Then he stood at the window and looked down across the field.

He didn't appreciate what he saw.

Naked people.

Utter fools.

And Skip out there already with his camera.

It was a poor combination.

11

IT WAS DARK with Cherry busy with some of the guests in the living room and there was nothing for him to do. At least there wasn't anything for him to do in the house but he knew what he had to do. What was right. Or as much as he could of what was right.

Monday…

They wouldn't be on the farm after that. She'd hand him the pictures but he'd decline to look at them. He'd burn them and they'd pack. On the way through town he'd list the farm for sale with some real estate broker, telling the man to get what he could for the place. Of course they'd have money but he wouldn't worry about it being spent. There were jobs and he'd find one. He always had. He'd make her happy.

At nine he went out to the Ford and started it. Apparently one of the plugs had gone bad and there was a miss to the motor. He felt in his pocket for a blank check as he drove out to the road. He had it all right and while he might have to lie to Cherry about what he had done with the thing, or where the money had gone, he couldn't leave the mountain as a man and not help Penny.

As a man…

In a sense, it was rather cruel and misguided thought that he was a man. Cliff Horton hadn't amounted to much but, giving the fellow credit, he had married her and given the child a name. It was more than he was doing.

Love…

His broad shoulders lifted and fell. The only love that was real to him was with that beautiful girl on the farm, a lovely creature who filled the nights with passion and mounting thrills.

Love…

Once before, a long time ago, with Penny. Yes, that had been love, too. Not a false love but a love crowded with respect and the wonderful experience of just being together.

He began to sweat.

Perhaps he would never meet the child, would someday die without knowing what the child was like. It was a lonely, helpless feeling that ripped at him as violently as a mountain lion bringing down an innocent lamb. Yet —

Well, a man had to decide, didn't he? He had his own life to live, didn't he? Of course. Everybody made mistakes and not all of them could be corrected. The mistake had been his — and hers. The child would be born of sin, in sin, exist in a sin over which the child had no control.

It was a nice night but cloudy, the moon partially obscured in the overcast. More rain? No doubt. It was the time of the year for that. The farmers prayed for it and the construction workers hated it. Few things, if any, pleased everybody. Not all females pleased all men.

Sex…

A powerful, thundering force. From it came joy and misfortune, such as the joy he had known with Penny and the misfortune which was hers to carry practically alone. Naturally, he'd send her money but that didn't make up for an absent husband and father. When you got right down to it there was nothing cheaper than money. Money was the convenient way out of difficulties.

He thought about leaving the farm and he knew that he'd miss it. He'd missed it in Iceland but there wasn't any financial promise in attempting to work the tired soil. If it hadn't been for the sale of fishing permits his parents would have failed. The only thing the ground was good for was to some rich man who could look at the grass and not be concerned about income.

There was a light in Penny's shack and he drove in, parking beside it. As he got out of the car he didn't know exactly what he was going to say or how he would put the words together but he had to say something. What he said to her that night had to last them forever.

He walked to the door, knocked and waited. It did feel like rain. What if it did rain? What if the people went back to the city early? Would they have to refund any of the money? He gave the issue no further consideration. Frankly, he didn't want that kind of cash.

She opened the door and her eyes lifted to his face, inquiring. She wore a blue robe, belted about her middle. He smiled at her but her lips remained in a firm, straight line.

"You must be lost," she said.

"Hardly."

"You were in a terrible hurry to get out of here the last time."

"That wasn't the last time. This is."

"Really?"

He pushed past her into the living room. He noticed an empty liquor bottle sitting on an end table and he was curious about that. She enjoyed a little beer but she had never been one to take to the bottle. Once more his guilt returned. Where had he shoved her? Just how much of her had he destroyed?

She closed the door as he sat down on the sofa but she remained standing. Again he glanced at the liquor bottle. There were two glasses beside it, empty. He frowned. Company? Why should it matter to him?

"Does that girl know you came here?" she asked.

"No."

"Cheat," she said with contempt.

"That didn't even enter my mind."

"I'll bet it didn't."

"Bet any way you like."

"I certainly will." She moved then and dropped down into a chair with a faded blue cover. "It's a long fall off the top of the mountain."

"Nobody's falling."

"Nobody except you."

"If I do fall I'll land on my feet."

"Or your head."

He stretched his long legs. Coming down to see her had been slightly foolish. He could have sent the check in the mail. There in the kitchen he had almost decided to do it that way but he had wanted to look at her again. She wasn't just a part of his past. She was almost all of it, the dreams of their youth, many of them unspoken, flowing constantly toward the rapids which had them forced apart.

"There's going to be a hospital bill," he said. "A hospital bill and you'll have to pay the doctor."

"I saw the doctor today."

"What did he tell you?"

"Not to worry about his money."

"But you do?"

"Yes. Wouldn't anybody? I was in debt before and you don't know how hard I worked to get out of it. Nothing comes easy but if you think it does you're stupid."

"I'm not stupid, Penny."

That caused her to smile. It was a bitter smile.

"The sad thing is you don't know just how stupid you are," she said. "You had more brains in first grade than you've got now."

"Your compliment is appreciated." He jerked his head in the direction of the bottle. "Nice that you found yourself a friend."

"I wouldn't call him that."

"But you drank with him."

"I threw mine out after he was gone. He drank the rest."

"A glutton, huh?"

"No. The bottle wasn't full."

"Anything serious with him?"

She began to pout.

"Don't be funny, Dutch. Could I be serious about anybody in my condition?"

"Some guys don't care."

"He wouldn't. He's the one who developed and sold those pictures of me."

Dutch leaned forward, tense, his elbows on his knees.

"That fellow I want to meet."

"Why?"

"Because I do."

"Then go and find him."

"Where?"

"I don't know. I didn't ask him and he didn't say. Somebody told him where I lived and he drove out here. In fact, you just missed him. He brought a bottle along and he asked me to pose for him. He said others have and he wouldn't sell any more pictures of me locally if I did. I told him to plaster the town with them but I still wouldn't do it. The girls who want to do those things have every right to do what they want but I'm not one of them. He said —"

"Yes?"

Her eyes went over his face like a speeding car with a reckless driver behind the wheel. Suddenly her eyes collided with his and locked.

"Never mind, Dutch."

"Hell, I care about this plenty."

"Do you? I don't think so because of her but if you do care it's up to you." Without warning, she choked down a sob. "I love you, you big lug. I love you all the way and always. Only I won't trade what I think to get what I want. When I gave you everything a girl can give a man it was without reservations. I even tried working at the farm to be near you, to help you, but I left after I saw it wouldn't do any good. You're old enough to know the difference between right and wrong. Nobody can show you that if it isn't inside of you. I — yes, I can see the need for a nudist colony. If there are people who feel they must follow the practice there has to be somewhere for them to go. But why cheapen it, Dutch, and turn the belief of many into a rotten sewer? And why be a party to it?"

"I don't care for the arrangement either," he admitted.

"But she — that Cherry — she's got you going and coming, hasn't she?"

He glanced down at his hands. They formed two giant fists.

"Some things you can't avoid, Penny."

"No, I guess not. We don't always do what we intend to do."

"I'm glad you understand." He reached into his pocket. "I'll leave you a check. It's a start and I'll send money every week. I'll —"

He stopped talking as he heard her get up and walk to the bedroom door.

"Keep your money," she said distantly. "I'd take your money if you were mine, all mine, but I don't want it any other way. I'm afraid but I'm not defeated. I'm proud of our love, that something wonderful can come from it. The mistake was more mine than yours because I let you. I'm mature and I don't deny it. People say ugly things about me but I'm not afraid. I'll live them down. You're the fool, blind and blundering. Maybe I love you but I couldn't marry a man who didn't know what he was himself. You think I'm the weaker sex. Take a ride and decide for yourself who is the weaker between the two of us. Take a ride and —"

She stepped into the bedroom and slammed the door shut behind her. He made no effort to follow her. He merely got up from the sofa and left the shack.

For a long time he sat outside in his car, thinking.

Skip Bart...

Carrying a camera and a gun...

Only a madman walked into the spitting muzzle of a gun. No matter how big or how strong you were you went down. You went down and stayed down and sometimes they buried you.

He drove toward town. Cherry would be busy at the farm and he wanted those photos of Penny off the market. If she wouldn't take his money it was the least he could do for her. A girl who sold herself to the camera had nothing to complain about but it was quite another matter with Penny. Twice she had gotten herself that way without benefit of marriage but it didn't have to follow that she was a bad girl. The first time she hadn't known what she was doing — he believed that now — and this with him had been the result of her search for love. Few people would pin a medal on either one of them for that but those things happened.

Of course he didn't know where the photographer lived but as soon as he got into town he consulted a phone book. The better shops would be closed at this time of the night but a man worked out of his cellar might be home and answer the phone.

Since Cranston was a small place there weren't many people in that kind of a business and he began at the top of the list. Not until the fourth call did he crack through silence.

"Hello," a male voice said. "Downs' Fotos."

"Yeah." Dutch grinned. "How far down can you go?"

"Huh? You some kind of a nut?"

"I just asked."

"I know that, fellow. Who are you?"

"A buyer. Somebody told me you sold nude photos. Anything to that?"

The photographer laughed.

"Well, in that case I can go pretty far down. When you get to the bottom of the barrel kick it out and you'll find me underneath."

Dutch nodded thoughtfully.

"I'll pay good for some nice shots."

"How good?"

"Let me see them and I'll tell you."

"I — all right. You got the address?"

"I should have. I've got the telephone book in front of me."

"Okay. It's the side door, leading into the cellar." There was another laugh. "I have a pic that's the best you'll ever see but it's not for sale. I don't sell what's personal."

"You name the deal."

Dutch hung up and left the phone booth, bumped into a little girl with a saucy smile on his way out to the car. The shop was on Broome Street, which wasn't a very good location. Broome Street was noted for the people who sucked their living out of the welfare department and the careless girls who left the street to roam the park. Not many small cities had a slum problem but there was one in Cranston. The factory jobs didn't pay enough to encourage people to work. The low pay drained them of ambition, made them lazy.

It wasn't difficult for him to locate Broome Street but he had a little trouble finding the building. The street lights were miserable and none of the places were marked. He had to count the houses from the corner, using odd numbers for that side, and the building turned out to be a three story brick structure. A weak bulb glowed toward the rear of the building and he guessed that was where the man had his shop. He didn't see how a person could make much money with such an arrangement but, in a sense, perhaps it wasn't too strange. This Downs didn't have any big store rent to pay and if he didn't earn his living by selling nudes he could always bang on doors and take pictures of kids. Most parents were suckers for that pitch.

He got out of the car and moved toward the light. There was some junk in the yard and he stepped on an empty can, almost falling. He felt his leg twist and the sharp stab of pain. But he didn't stop. It took a lot to bother him. He could go down in a fight, struggle to his knees and nearly tear a man's guts out with his fists. His father had taught him not to start a fight unless it was necessary but to be sure that he finished it. Some men had discovered he had learned his lesson well.

He descended the steps, pushed open the door and walked inside without knocking. His weight was on the balls of his feet, the muscles in his arms and shoulders drawing up tight. For some reason he felt that he had no time to waste, that he had too much to do. The only thing was that he didn't know just what he was going to do.

"I'm Downs," a redhead said. "You must be the guy who's busting out with the cash."

Downs was about thirty, tall and powerfully built. He was stripped to the waist and sweat covered his chest. He had an ugly face with a scar on one cheek and eager, probing eyes.

"If you've got what I want, yes."

The studio, if it could be called that, didn't seem much but of course Dutch couldn't see it all. Curtains separated the rear section from the front. The only two things in this space where he stood was a desk and a small counter.

"It isn't a big selection," Downs informed him. "But it's hot."

"Show me."

"Sure. They're on the counter. Pick out what you want and tell me how many prints. Then we'll set the price."

Dutch crossed to the counter. There were a number of photos and he recognized some of the girls. They had visited the farm but Skip Bart had neglected to tell him about this. He was of the opinion that the girls, no matter what they were, hadn't consented to be used in such a manner. There were nude studies which could be purchased that were works of art but these pictures were rotten and degrading.

"This one," he said and picked up the photo of Penny.

"You're passing up better items."

"Am I? I should go to jail?"

"I can fix them."

"Fine, but I don't care what you can do. This girl appeals to me and I'll pay high for the negative."

"I don't sell negatives."

"How much?"

"I told you I don't sell them. Anyway I'm going to use her more and more but I need the negative to force her. Lives in a shack and thinks she's so damned nice."

Dutch put the picture aside for the moment.

"You had a special you were going to let me look at," he reminded Downs.

Downs stepped behind the counter. He leered and reached beneath it. The eagerness in his eyes had turned to lust.

"I do some work for a guy," he said. "Delicate work you might say — men and girls together. I don't get the drift but I charge and I get paid. Things like that would bring me in a fortune but I'll play along with him if he keeps his word. Oh, not his word maybe. His promise."

"And the promise?"

"Stuff."

"That figures."

Downs' leer became more pronounced. He didn't act drunk but Dutch decided he must be onto something. Perhaps the needle or a reefer. If he had cared less he wouldn't have cared at all. It was simply that nobody could tell what a man in this condition would do.

"Stuff," Downs repeated. "A couple of nights with this and I'll find myself on the ceiling. I've seen a hundred dames, probably more, but none like her. Do you blame me?"

Dutch fingered the photograph that was handed to him. Shock and resentment filled him. His head pounded for a second, then stopped. He noticed his hands. They were shaking, his palms damp.

Cherry.

Wearily, he shook off the vision of this man with her. He couldn't believe it. The girl he loved, letting Skip do this to her, trading her flesh as he would a used car.

"The Princess," that girl near the lake had said one day.

He hadn't thought of it until now but what did it mean. He knew, coldly, what it could mean but once more he refused to believe. She wouldn't. Never. Not with this man or with any man. She came to him in the night and she was his.

"Try not to start a fight," his father had said.

No, don't start a fight. Refuse to swing first. Let the other guy jar you and then bury him in his own blood. Double him up with a hard one to the stomach and follow this up by taking out some of his teeth with a solid right.

"Creep!" he shouted, unable to control himself.

The counter wasn't fastened to the floor and he hurled it from between them. Alarmed, the red-head attempted to say something, to protest, but whatever it was died in his throat as Dutch smashed him full in the face. Downs stumbled against the curtain, muttering curses, then took the curtain with him as he fell to the floor.

"Fellow," Dutch warned. "Fellow, you'd better fight."

He untangled Downs from the curtain and jerked the guy to his feet. He held him this time, not letting him drop, and powered another right to the area where blood was beginning to show on Downs' mouth.

"The negative," he said. "Of Penny. The negative or I hammer you through the wall."

He caught one of the redhead's arms and started to twist it, all of his savage strength going into the effort. Calmly, deliberately he bent Downs to his knees, used his own knee as he brought it up under Downs' chin.

Downs begged and moaned but Dutch refused to give him relief. The photographer's arm was now completely out of shape, going further out of shape as Dutch applied tremendous pressure to the bone that would soon snap.

"Please!" Downs managed to say, now desperate, suffering.

"Where is it?"

"Back — there."

"Where?"

"Back —"

Dutch dragged him past a curtain to a small metal filing cabinet. Downs gasped with pain and clawed with his free hand at the air. A brutal knee to the chin ended his misery and Dutch let go of him. The redhead slumped to the floor, spitting blood for a moment and then lay still.

It only took Dutch a couple of minutes to remove all of the negatives from the files. He glanced through them, found the one of Penny, grunted and placed them in a pile on the concrete floor. A second later he struck a match to the assortment of filth and watched with satisfaction as the negatives shot up in flames.

As soon as the fire died he turned his attention to the man lying in front of the filing cabinet. He had an inhuman urge to smash in the man's ribs, to leave him a broken mass of bone and flesh.

But he didn't.

He was running as he left the cellar and plunged outside into the night.

Only part of his job was done.

The rest was still to come.

12

HE DROVE TOWARD the farm like a maniac just released from a straight jacket. And he swore, bitterly, wildly. Regardless of what he did with the car the motor kept missing. Still, there was no use swearing. He couldn't do anything about that plug or whatever it was which was causing the trouble. There was only one thing he could do much about and he was determined to do it.

Cherry…

Maybe he loved her the same as before but that photo Downs had shown him had cut him all the way through from his belly to his back — the photo plus the promise Skip had made. He couldn't understand the promise or why she would consent to such an affair, assuming she had consented, but he did understand the nude picture of her. She had posed for that type of stuff — this she hadn't denied — and there were bound to be shots of her floating around. This he had overlooked when she had told him but he realized as he drove that he had resented it, yet refusing to recognize the resentment. He thought this was natural enough. No man would want the girl he loved on public display.

He glanced at Penny's shack as he passed it. The violence he had displayed in town had been for her, to protect her, and he had the uncomfortable feeling that some portion of what he was belonged inside of that shack with her. No longer did he sense the need for revenge, to take her body and gloat because he had done so. More than Downs who had lay sprawled on the floor she had suffered to a far greater extent than she deserved. More —

That night with Cliff Horton, foolish and helpless…

A marriage that had been wrong from the start…

A child, innocent and dying without cause…

And failure…

Now another child, his child, the child of what he had thought to be revenge, and yet she loved him. Tragedy, stark and real.

Cherry…

He was confused, upset, furious about Skip Bart. He'd refuse the money paid, chase them all from the farm that night. He wanted nothing more to do with this sorry, unfortunate operation. Cherry would see his point of view, the decency that his parents had given him, and she would admire him for it. That construction job out of town — well, if not that one another one. Somewhere, somehow. Faith in each other, it would carry them along a straight and beautiful road.

Only a few lights were on in the house when he arrived at the farm. He parked the Ford, blocking a couple of cars, and jumped out.

Inside he found nobody on the lower floor so he climbed the stairs. Cherry was probably asleep, tired of waiting for him, her body delightful upon the big double bed. He'd awaken her with a kiss, reason with her, make her listen to all that was common sense. And he'd send a check to Penny. He had to do that.

Cherry wasn't in their room.

But there were voices down the hall.

He listened.

Skip Bart, his voice edged with ice.

Cherry's voice, amused, insulting.

And the fat man's voice, begging.

Without making any noise he walked through the hall. All of the doors were closed. Somebody laughed. Yes, the doors were closed although there weren't any locks on them. Closed so that two could enjoy the pleasures of forbidden love. Love on a counter with a price tag written all over it. He thought it amazing how far he had sunk, what he had permitted to exist in a house where love for his folks had once been a thing of beauty and mutual understanding.

The fat man's door was closed also but he could hear everything that was being said inside of the bedroom.

"I haven't got all night," Cherry complained. "Dutch won't be gone for long unless that slut down the road is better than I am."

"You stay," Skip told her crossly. "This is the killing I wanted and we've got it. The rest was peanuts. A grand here, two there. Can you play the ponies on that? Hell, you never picked a winner."

Dutch rocked back and forth and wiped the sweat from his forehead. He thought of going away with her on Monday and it suddenly lacked any meaning at all. Something was happening here that he didn't know about. The new sweat on his forehead became cold.

"Fifty thousand," the fat man was saying. "That's blackmail."

"Who asked you what it was?" Skip wanted to know. "You wanted the best of the lot and you had her. For what she gave you some across with fifty grand."

There was a short silence.

"Maybe a thousand," the fat man suggested. "Fifty thousand is too much."

"Is it? Mister, I took a lot of picture of you."

"I made sure his face was in it," Cherry added.

"Your wife would like a print of this," Skip said.

"You wouldn't!"

Skip's laugh was hollow.

"Who says I wouldn't? Not me, you fat slob. We've done well up here, or pretty good, but you were the toad we were out to nail. And, guy, you're nailed. Your hide's on the wall and your head has been cut off. Your wife would quit you tomorrow over this and you'd find yourself without a dime."

"Damn, and to think — "

"You should have thought before. Well, you didn't so start thinking now. I'll take your check but I keep the picture until the check clears the bank. As soon as that's done I'll deliver it to you and you've got nothing to worry about."

"The police — "

"Shut up. You can't go to the police and you know it. You haven't got the guts and it's our word against yours anyway. You're hooked. Brother, you're hooked proper. You're hooked like the sucker that you are."

There was a further discussion from inside of the room but Dutch didn't pay any attention to it. His mind was going back to the morning he'd met Cherry, to the girl of the night before, of being drunk and talking to Skip, to the bold hints that had come from a couple of the girls who visited the farm. The Princess. All of it there for him to see and he had seen none of it. Her glorious body, ready to meet his physical needs during the darkness of the night, losing himself in her passion, believing and loving her, trading Penny's love for a basket of nothing. Nothing. There was no doubt in his mind about that. Nothing but the shell surrounding an impossible dream, building hopes. And that business about him bringing her across a state line, breaking the law, her excuse that Skip held some strange power over her. False. A pack of lies, one lie creating another lie.

He was soaked with sweat. Maybe Skip had a gun and maybe he'd use it. Maybe somebody would die in that room. Others had died for less. Some men ran when they were cornered. Some killed blindly, without feeling, then regretted it when the law closed in on them.

The fat man…

Well, the fat man was only important as an individual. The important thing was the lying and the cheating, the utter stupidity that had been his. If he was meant to die before a blazing gun he'd rather do that than live with the memory of a sordid past.

He took a deep breath, not a breath of fear but of calm resolution as he considered his destiny for that night.

A panel of the door shattered as he kicked it open and lunged into the room.

He stopped just inside.

Skip had a gun all right. A small gun, pointing death at his chest.

Cherry was undressed and standing near the dresser. The fat man, also naked, sat on the edge of the bed. Skip was fully clothed and the camera lay on the floor near his feet.

"I had a feeling this would happen," Skip said in disgust. "We're on the big haul and here comes the clown."

"I didn't hear his car come in," Cherry protested.

"Who could? The driveway is on the other side of the house. I told you to get yourself down to his room but, no, you had to stay and see this thing through. Dames. What sense have they got?"

"It's my money, too. I earned it with that jerk."

"When did I ever cheat you?"

"Last year, at the other camp we had. More than once, Skip. A hell of a lot more than once. And during the winter, when you were chasing down the others. I never knew how much you really collected. All I got was a few bucks and the doubtful privilege of sleeping with you every night."

"Why wouldn't I sleep with you? We're married, aren't we?"

"Don't remind me. It's some marriage."

"Aw, drop dead. What are we going to do with this guy?" Her lips curled.

"I don't care what you do with him. He had his fun — but he is more of a man than you are."

Dutch measured the distance between himself and the gun. Too far but he couldn't change the distance. Most of those small guns weren't too accurate and he had to depend on that but there were a few things he had to know first.

Married…

A lousy thing…

All of it lousy…

"Clever," he said, feeling nothing but contempt for these two. "You were looking that night, weren't you? The night you talked with me?"

"I'm always looking," Skip agreed and grinned.

"You set it up."

"Of course. It wasn't difficult. You were just in off that plane and you had this farm. We had one last year but we couldn't go back again.

"Maybe."

"And you or Cherry followed me to that bar the next morning. It was perfect for you and your plans."

"Naturally. This honey can sell anybody on anything with her shape. She sold you, didn't she?"

"A nice way to use your own wife."

"Who worries? There's enough of her for everybody."

"You ought to know," Cherry said. "You've certainly made me very much available to any man who had the price." "Relax, will you? We close this up with the fat boy and we break off for Mexico. You read about that? Thirty bucks a month and you get a house with a cook and maid thrown in."

The fat man shifted his weight on the bed. He hadn't said anything since Dutch had entered the room. Now he wet his lips with the tip of his tongue. He did that twice and blinked his small eyes.

"This is terrible," he declared. "Fifty thousand is impossible. My wife would miss that amount of money."

Skip sneered.

"Tell her you lost it in the stock market."

Cherry laughed.

"What's the matter?" she wanted to know. "Wasn't the stock you bought worth a big wad of change?"

Dutch's muscles tensed. He knew all that he needed to know. He knew that Skip was a flesh merchant and that Cherry was no good. Strangely enough, the last didn't annoy him. She was beautiful, yes, but beyond that she was nobody, something less than a tramp. More than likely she recruited the girls for Skip and he led them down a path of despair. He knew now why Skip had talked to the men before they left the camp, why they were unspoken and sullen, why they never returned. He knew, too, that this didn't even resemble the nudist movement but that it was merely an old game played in a different way. Important or wealthy men had to pay in an effort to protect their jobs and reputations. As for the girls who shared in the blackmail plot they had nothing to lose. They were paid for their services and anything above that didn't concern them.

"A bullet in the belly for you," Skip said to Dutch.

He ignored Skip.

"Monday," he said to Cherry. "You sneaking bitch, you'll be sitting in jail on Monday."

"A bullet in the belly," Skip repeated and laughed harshly. "She's my wife and I caught you trying to rape her. You came at me, guy. The gun is licensed and I've got a right to carry it. I only shot you to protect myself. The fat man can't say anything different. I get his fifty grand and a solid witness. They'll believe me because you've got that girl down the road knocked up. So you had to have something new. They'll see you as a woman chaser, a man who would do anything for his pleasure. I go free and they shovel dirt over you. It's your own fault. In a couple of hours we'd been out of here. You weren't buying the idea of the camp and we couldn't last. But with fifty grand who has to last?"

Dutch didn't pause to wonder whether or not Skip could get away with murder. Seconds were precious, perhaps the final seconds during which he would live. He merely told himself that if he died he'd die going across that room.

He went, down low, all of his weight driving him, any fear that he might have had overshadowed by necessity.

A female scream of terror filled the room, sharp, penetrating.

But it wasn't as bad as the roar of the gun.

He felt the bullet slam into his shoulder rocking him slowing him for an instant. Then he had Skip's legs in his grasp upsetting the fellow as the gun went off again. He didn't feel anything that time as he dug furiously to gain possession of the gun. His arm was numb, his shoulder throbbing, but he groaned, fighting off the pain, and found the wrist which he sought. There was no mercy inside of him, only hate. Nor was there any mercy when he felt the wrist snap, heard the long cry of agony that was followed by a sob of complete defeat.

Dutch got up and carried the gun over to the fat man who sat on the bed.

"You watch them," he said thickly. "The rest is up to the police."

"But — "

"Do as I tell you, huh?"

"Well — all right."

The only other thing he did before he left the room was to remove the film from the camera, exposing it to the light, destroying any pictures that had been taken.

Reaching the police on the telephone was easy but his next call required somewhat more consideration.

"It's all over," he told Penny when she answered.

"Whats all over?" She sounded sleepy.

"Everything except — "

"Except what?"

"Except us."

"Us?" She was awake now. "Oh, if I could only believe that!"

"You can believe it."

He hung up and started for the stairs.

He didn't quite make them.

Exhausted, feeling the loss of blood, he slumped into a chair.

A price, he thought.

Everything had it.

13

THE WORK WAS hard but Dutch enjoyed it. Construction work was usually hard but this job was a lot different than the one in Iceland. At least when he quit for the day, tired and dirty, he had somewhere to go, somebody — two somebodies — waiting for him.

"Steel," one of the men said to him. "Don't you ever get sick of it?"

"Why should I? You can't build much without it."

"And the shoulder?"

"Sore."

Of course the shoulder still bothered him but the doctor said that it would get better in time. Sun, the doctor said. Sun helped. Maybe. Anyway he got plenty of it on the job and weekends.

However, the weekends were the best, not counting the love he found with Penny in the trailer at night. Weekends they went to a nudist camp, a decent one, and it was a happy family affair. No sex or blackmail, just clean living in the company of nice people. Gone were his former inhibitions and even the baby had an extremely healthy look to him. Penny had been slow to approve but now she was as much an addict as he was.

He tried not to think about Skip Bart or Cherry but sometimes he did. He supposed it was inevitable because the past was always there, a constant reminder of both success and failure. Their racket had been smashed and they were each doing long terms in prison. Downs had entered the nude photo field again but he had made the mistake of selling his pictures in the wrong spot. For this he had found a hard cot in a cell where there weren't any girls. As for the fat man he had become involved in the smut of Skip's and Cherry's trial and although his wife hadn't divorced him he couldn't spend a dime unless he accounted for it.

Dutch guessed he had been lucky with the farm. A broker from the city had purchased it for a fair price, the trailer and a new car was paid for and they had money in the bank. But more than anything else they had each other, a son who added beauty to their love, and he felt that any man who asked for more was a fool.

Every afternoon at five he left the job, raced three miles to where the trailer was located, met Penny's waiting lips with his crushing mouth and showered immediately.

"The boy's asleep," she often said as he stepped from the shower.

Then, pleased, he would look at her nude figure, grin and ask the same question he always asked when the moment was right.

"And dinner?"

Her smile of invitation would reach up into his eyes.

"I know you're hungry only I thought — "

Generally he was hungry but he was aware of what she thought without being told.

Anyway he couldn't see her, willing and anxious, and not think the same thing.

Or do all that he could about it.

Which is exactly what he did.

Whenever the boy slept.

Fortunately, the boy slept a lot.

WOLFBAIT
UNDER THE COUNTER CULTURE

ALSO AVAILABLE BY ORRIE HITT

Nudist Camp
Orrie Hitt's classic novel in which paradise comes with a price.

THE STEPHEN GLASS COLLECTION

Amazons of Yesteryear
A rare, action-packed collection of images of
wrestling women of the 1940s and 1950s.

Beauty Off-Duty
Relaxed, everyday moments caught on camera.

Naked in the Menagerie
A playful look at Eve accompanied by her animal friends.

Nudist Camp Follies – volumes 1 and 2
An intimate look at the natural
and free atmosphere in Sun Clubs.

Nymphs and Naiads
Beauty unadorned and outdoors.

Poise and Pose
A magnificent series of photographs
of female beauty taken in the studio.

THE EVA GRANT COLLECTION

The Glamour Camera of Eva Grant
A short biography of Eva Grant, one of the world's foremost
female figure photographers of the 1950s and 1960s, accompanied
by a selection of some of her most enticing work.

Line and Form
A nostalgic review of Eva Grant's
glamour magazine of the 1950s.

Glamour Model Revue
Featuring June Palmer, Paula Page and Tina Madison.

THE WILLIAM WELBY COLLECTION

**Naked and Unashamed:
Nudism from Six Points of View**
William Welby's initial impressions of nudism.

The Naked Truth about Nudism
William Welby gets to bare all in this first hand
exploration of British Naturism.

It's Only Natural: The Philosophy of Nudism
William Welby's musings on getting back to nature
and the tyranny of fashion.

Naked as Nature Intended
The epic tale of a nudist picture by Pamela Green,
with photographs by Douglas "Dambuster" Webb, DFM.

The Naked Truth About Harrison Marks
The notorious biography by Franklyn Wood.

Slide Show
A luscious look at the photographic
slides of Harrison Marks.

Past Masters of the Nude
An illustrated bibliography of nude photography books
published in England from 1896 to 1960.

Doing Rude Things
The history of the British sex film.

Cinema au Naturel
A history of nudist film.

Sauna for Beginners
A Pocket Guide.

Miniten: Rules of the Game
Invented in the 1930s, Miniten is a
tennis-like game played by naturists.

X-ray Specs and Other Vintage Ads
A unique treasure chest of vintage advertising,
full of tease and prurient silliness.

Receive a **FREE** copy of
How to Take Glamour Studies by Harrison Marks
when you sign up to our mailing list at
www.pamela-green.com/free-book